To Love a
HIGHLAND
Rogue

Heart of a Scot Book One

COLLETTE CAMERON

Blue Rose Romance™
Portland, Oregon

Sweet-to-Spicy Timeless Romance™

To Love a Highland Rogue
Heart of a Scot Series, Book One
Copyright © 2017 Collette Cameron
Cover Design by: Teresa Spreckelmeyer

Blue Rose Romance™
8420 N Ivanhoe #83054
Portland, Oregon 97203

ISBN PRINT: 9781944973506

www.collettecameron.com

"Ah, my love, my precious love. All will be well, I vow. Somehow I will make it so."

Other Collette Cameron Books

A Waltz with a Rogue Novella Series
A Kiss for Miss Kingsley
Bride of Falcon
Her Scandalous Wish
To Tame a Scoundrel's Heart
The Wallflower's Wicked Wager

Castle Brides Series
The Viscount's Vow
Highlander's Hope
The Earl's Enticement

Conundrums of the Misses Culpepper Series
Brooke: Wagers Gone Awry
Blythe: Schemes Gone Amiss
Brette: Intentions Gone Astray

Highland Heather Romancing a Scot Series
Triumph and Treasure
Virtue and Valor
Heartbreak and Honor
Scandal's Splendor

Seductive Scoundrels
A Diamond for a Duke

Heart of a Scot Series
To Love a Highland Rogue

A Scottish Short Story
Heart of a Highlander

Boxed Sets
Embraced by a Rogue
To Love a Reckless Lord

Dedication

To my darling Grandpa Cameron from whom I

borrowed my *nom de plume*

I share your love of song birds, tea,

and adoration of all things Scottish.

Till we meet again—

Acknowledgements

To *Love a Highland Rogue* wouldn't have been written if Kathryn Le Veque hadn't graciously asked me to be a part of *The Forbidden Highlands* anthology.

Honored and delighted to be in such pristine company as Eliza Knight, Terri Brisbin, Amy Jarecki and other wonderful authors, I couldn't refuse.

And as my muse often does, it went bezerk and decided I needed to launch a new series, with *To Love a Highland Rogue* as the first book in my **Heart of a Scots** series.

As always, I must thank my amazing editor, Danielle Fine and my cover artist Theresa Spreckelmeyer. And I must humbly thank Kathryn Le Veque for *To Love a Highland Rogue's* cover quote.

xoxo

Prologue

Dunrangour Tower, Scottish Highlands
6 September, 1701

"Logan, my boy, ye sign here." Artair Rutherford pointed to an empty space below his and laird Roderick Findlay's bold, slanted signature.

Ach, cow turds.

Despite his frustration, Logan obediently propped his battered toy sword against the table's leg, and after carefully dipping the quill into the inkwell, lifted his uncertain gaze to his father.

"Me full name, Da?"

"Aye, son."

"And when I do, it means I must wed her? When I'm a mon?" He pointed the quill at a wee lassie in an elaborate wooden cradle, gnawing on her wet fist.

"Aye, lad." Inclining his head, Da patted Logan's shoulder, the gesture more prodding than reassuring. "She'll be yer wife."

Logan sucked in his cheeks and crimped his mouth. "I dinna want to get married."

What need have I for a wife? Da disna have one.

"It's a good match. A brilliant one, truth to tell." Bending over a little, Da peered intently into his eyes. "But more importantly, son, the union benefits Scotland."

Findlay, Dunrangour's giant of a laird, snorted loud as a draft horse and shook his shaggy blond mane. "So say some."

Logan gulped and took a reflexive step backward.

"Ever heard such a colossal *jobby* before, Fergus and Hamish?" Findlay bit out, his jaw muscles jumping.

Such a pile of shite?
Which part?

The stupid match or the benefitin' Scotland part?

A pair of Dunrangour clansmen acting as witnesses, their flinty gazes unyielding and faces granite hard, grunted and smirked in agreement.

"And o' course, Mayra's dowry—particularly the land portion—be of nae interest to ye, be it, Rutherford? But, ye cannae touch either yet, can ye? No' until our children actually wed. And then it'll be the lad's to do with as he pleases, no' yers. How that must set yer teeth on edge and stick in yer greedy craw."

Findlay's low chuckle, more sinister than humorous, filled the tense silence. Satisfaction, or mayhap even gloating, tinged his words and ignited his vivid blue eyes.

Viking eyes.

Da said Dunrangour's laird was descended from the barbaric Norsemen, and Logan could well believe it.

"Asinine requirin' me to provide half of the lass's marriage settlement now. Reeks of extortion." Findlay's hefty glower encompassed Da and Mr. Hyde,

3

the king's agent.

Logan scrunched his forehead and mouth, gazing between the angry laird and his gentle lady.

Didn't they want this troth thing either?

As a lad, he couldn't disobey Da's order, but they were grown-ups. And adults could do what they wanted.

Why didn't they just say no then?

Reddish brows drawn into such a severe vee they almost touched, Da glared hard at Findlay until Logan's tugging on his coat finally drew his father's attention.

"What's a cowry, Da?"

"Dowry." His father's stern features softened a wee bit. "It's a token promisin' ye and the lass will wed."

A sneer curled Findlay's mouth as he crossed his thick arms and planted a bulging shoulder against the fireplace. "I'd call it extortion and a forced match between a wee six-year-old lad and an infant lass."

"Give careful thought to yer words, Findlay. Some might consider them and yer attitude treasonous. Ye wouldn't want a hint of anythin' untoward to reach His Majesty's ears." Mr. Hyde, *tsked* disapprovingly, his eyes gone squinty and suspicious. His pointy nostrils even twitched in reproach.

Like a giant wharf rat.

Logan pinched his nose and pointed his face away. Reeking of dirty feet, stale sweat, and rotting teeth, the agent stank worse than Leith's docks.

"Go ahead, sign," Da urged Logan. "We needs be on our way."

Mutiny pounded against Logan's ribs, and he thrust out his lower lip.

Something about this didn't feel right—made him slightly afraid and his tummy waffy.

Like when he awoke during the middle of the night and the castle was too quiet. Too ghostly and strange. And he lay alone in his chamber with only his sword and a carved dog for protection. Too scared to move or get up, but just as terrified to stay buried beneath the weighty bedcoverings.

"Why do *I* have to marry her? Why cannae someone else?" Logan veered the fretting bairn a troubled glance, and leaning toward Da, whispered, "She's no' verra bonnie."

"Yer king asks it of ye, lad. As do I." Da indicated where Logan should sign again.

So he must marry a strawberry-faced, slobbering baby for a prissy king he'd never met?

Unfair!

Logan wasn't supposed to swear, but he could *think* oaths with no one the wiser. And right now, he wanted to think whole bunches of them.

Bloody hell. Blister and damn. God's toenails.

Bampot. Diddy. Scunner.

Shite. Shite. Shite!

What would Da do if Logan stomped his feet and hollered, "Nae," at the top of his voice or threw the quill on the floor, mashing it beneath his foot, cursing all the while?

If he was required to wed that red-faced bairn, shouldn't he have something in return?

Hmm...

Maybe...

"Can I have a puppy then?" Logan skewed a

hopeful brow and chewed the side of his lower lip.

He really, *really* wanted a puppy, but Da always stalled, saying mayhap when he was older. And older never, ever ... *ever* came.

Logan squared his shoulders and jutted his chin. "If'n I be old enough to become—"*What was the word?*—"be...trussed, then I'm old enough to have me own dog."

"Be-trothed," Mr. Hyde muttered beneath his breath, stressing each syllable. "The word is *Be. Trothed.* And the nerve of the lad. Askin' for a mongrel when he should be thankin' His Majesty for the honor he's bestowed upon the boy."

Mr. Hyde shook his head and *tsked* reproachfully again.

Showed what the cranky auld tosspot knew, comparing honor to a puppy. Lads didn't play with honor. Or have it curl up in their beds and keep them warm. Or lick their giggling faces until they gasped for air.

Logan held his breath, afraid Da would say no. Again.

But this time Da laughed, his smile folding his face clear to the corners in amusement, and even Findlay's lips twitched a mite.

"Aye, ye can have yer puppy. Now sign the document. We need to depart soon if we're to make the first lodgin' house before nightfall." Dad closed the dowry chest's lid, and after securing the lock, tucked the key into his sporran.

Logan murmured each of his five names, Logan Greer Wallace Robert Rutherford, as he laboriously wrote them, remembering to carefully shape the letters as his tutor demanded. Only the nib scritching against the crisp parchment and the bairn's coos interrupted the eerie calm entombing the great hall.

Once he'd finished, Mr. Hyde all but snatched the quill from Logan's hand and proceeded to scribble his name, sprinkle sand atop the ink, and lastly, affix a fancy seal to the scarlet wax at the bottom.

"Can I play with Coburn now, Da?"

Beaming in a very pleased way Logan had never seen before, his father dipped his square chin.

"As soon as ye say yer farewells and give the lass

the gift ye brought, ye can play with yer cousin."

Logan opened his pouch, and sticking his tongue between his teeth, fished around in his sporran for the pin. He'd assumed it was a present for Lady Findlay when Da asked him to carry the heart-shaped, crown-topped token. Once he'd pulled the piece free, he turned it over and picked out a bit of fuzz—probably from his plaid—from the bright blue stone in the center.

"It matches her eyes." He extended the Luckenbooth brooch.

The bairn snatched it from his hand and promptly stuffed the scrolled end into her mouth. However, Lady Findlay gently took the clasp from her daughter.

"Nae, sweeting. Ye'll hurt yerself."

Her voice sounded funny and tight, as if she tried not to cry.

Grabbing his wooden sword, Logan made to join Coburn. Barely one year older and often mistaken for his twin, his cousin was also his best friend.

"Logan?" Lady Findlay's lyrical voice stopped him.

Holy rotten haddock.

What now?

Eager to find Coburn, and slay all manner of mythical beasts from dragons to trows, Logan fingered the sword's smooth hilt and slowly faced her.

"M'lady?"

Her ladyship offered him a brave, if somewhat wobbly smile.

"I ken ye be young, and ye dinna fully understand what has transpired here today. But I ask ye to be kind to Mayra, to no' hurt her—to keep her from harm. And someday, perhaps, ye can come to love her. Can ye promise me that, Logan?"

After coming to stand before Lady Findlay, he cocked his head.

"Aye, m'lady. I surely can."

Bracing his hands on his upright sword, Logan peered into the cradle.

Covered in lacy stuff, the infant gurgled, waved her chubby fists, and blinked her big blue eyes. Whitish bumps covered her face, and drool ran from one corner of her slobbery mouth.

Och.

He pinched his features tighter.

"Why's her face all puckered? And riddy and blotchy?" He touched his own smooth cheeks while eyeing her doubtfully. "Are ye sure the bairn is a lassie? She has nae hair."

Just like Mr. Hyde—bald as a stone or a goose egg.

"Aye, Mayra is a lass." Lady Findlay lifted the wee one from the cradle, and after arranging the bairn on her lap, brushed her fingers across the lass's head. "She's fair, like her father. It may take a while, but she'll have hair. Would ye like to hold her?"

Nae!

Logan shook his head and backed away. Horror of horrors. He'd rather cuddle a selkie or a kelpie. He never wanted to hold or touch the wriggling bairn.

Ever.

"I would have an oath from ye too, lad." Findlay went to one muscled knee before him, and still Logan had to crane his neck to meet the laird's eyes.

By jiminy, he's huge. Way bigger than Da.

"Court my wee lass beforehand," Findlay said. "And wait until she's passed her twentieth birthday to wed."

"Now see here," Mr. Hyde spluttered, his eyebrows writhing like great, giant, fuzzy gray worms. "That's no' part of the settlement."

"Nae age nor courtship restrictions were specified, Hyde. Sloppy on yer part." Findlay's frigid smile nailed the nasty wee man to the hall's paneled wall.

Dunrangour's laird leaned in and whispered in Logan's ear. "And when ye are an adult, and if'n ye dinna want to marry Mayra, petition the monarchy to grant ye a reprieve. I shall ask, too, if that's what ye want. But ye needs return her dowry else she cannae marry another."

Logan veered a brief glance to the squirming infant. Not have to marry that blotchy-faced lass? Aye, that Logan could promise.

"Sir, it shall be as ye request."

1

Outside Glenliesh Village, Near Dunrangour Tower
12 March 1720

Mayra grinned at the days-old dun calves frolicking in the meadow, which gleamed as if blanketed with enormous emeralds. Early-blooming Lady's Smock added faint lilac patches here and there. And if she weren't mistaken, a few bluebells already bobbed their cheerful heads amongst the green bordering the Windlespoons' estate.

She wouldn't stop and say hello to her dearest friend, Gaira, today. Gaira's doting parents had whisked her to Edinburgh for the Social Season, something Mayra would never experience.

Envy tried to jab her, but she resolutely tamped the dark sentiment down and focused on the lovely day instead.

After a surprisingly mild, if typically wet winter, spring had blossomed prematurely this year. As she expertly guided the dog cart along the muddy, rutted path still dotted with puddles from last night's blustery showers, Mayra smiled for the sheer joy of the sun's stroking rays and the vivid azure sky peeping between the ever-present silver-tinted clouds.

These were the days when she relished the Highlands; when spring promised new life, fresh hope, and possibly, even a wee romping adventure.

Och, so wonderful, if only it might be so.

She detested the rain—almost a treasonous attitude for a Scot.

Yet the dampness, as well as everything cloaked in grayish hues from palest ash to deepest charcoal—day after day, weeks on end—wore on her.

Especially since her only regular reprieve from the keep—also pewter-colored from its corbelling and crow-stepped gables to its corner turrets and bartizans—were these twice-weekly visits to the village.

Always—*always, God's teeth*—accompanied by someone.

Usually a clan member, one or two of her rapscallion teenage brothers, or Mayra's diligent middling-aged maid, Bettie. On rare occasions, dear Mum joined Mayra, but since Da died two years ago, those instances had grown fewer and fewer.

The latter pairs' keen regard seldom left her longer than a minute, so seriously did they take her chaperonage. Consequently, nothing the least bit exciting ever occurred on the jaunts. Unless Mayra counted her brothers' penchant for regularly becoming embroiled in mischief of some sort in the village.

Today, Bettie sat in the dog cart's rear seat, food baskets for the needy tucked inside the rectangular box beneath her. She snored softly as Mayra skillfully guided Horace, their mild-tempered going-to-fat gelding, along the well-worn, rutted path passing for a road.

"I promised Maggi MacPherson I'd stop in for a

short visit and share a pot of tea today after I deliver the baskets. Do ye want to go with me, Bettie? Or would ye rather take a cup with yer sister, and I can collect ye afterward?"

Mayra spared a swift glance behind her.

Chin drooping, Bettie dozed, her cream kerchief-covered head bouncing with each jar of the cart. She stirred and blinked sleepily while yawning behind her hand.

"I'd like to see ye to the inn and then walk to Agnes's, but I'm feelin' a wee bit waff." She sneezed and blinked watery eyes. "If ye promise no' to be more than a half an hour, Mayra, I suppose ye can see yerself there this one time. Straight to The Dozin' Stag and back, ye hear? Nae dawdlin' or givin' anyone cause to wag their tongue."

Did anyone ever need cause to blether?

Not in Mayra's limited experience.

"I dinna dawdle, as ye well ken. Besides, I cannae imagine what could occur in such a short time that would raise even a single eyebrow hair."

"*Hmph.*" Bettie made a mollified sound before

sneezing again. Her plum-round cheeks slightly flushed, she pulled her shawl snugger. "And let's be keepin' it that way, shall we?"

Arching an indignant brow, Mayra directed her attention back to the road as the neat village loomed ahead. Honestly, a little tittle-tattle on her behalf might prove most invigorating, given her wholly predictable and dull-as-a-worn-quill's life.

However, Bettie did appear a trifle peaked. Rather wan about her mouth, too.

Swallowing her disappointment, Mayra released a slow sigh.

Nae loitering in the village today.

After she made her excuses to Maggi, she'd see Bettie home and to her bed as quickly as possible. She'd take no chances with her beloved servant's health.

An hour later, having delivered food baskets to Widow Ainsley, the kind but dotty Pinkerton sisters, Dunrangour's deaf-as-a-turnip retired gardener, and four more to the kirk for other villagers in need, she drew the equipage before the MacPherson's charming three-story lodging house.

Nearly a century of weather had worn the stone surface to a welcoming mellow, tawny-slate, a delightful contrast to the faded paint-chipped poppy-red shutters.

As always, mouth-watering smells wafted from within, and Mayra's stomach gurgled in anticipation of enjoying one of Maggi MacPherson's Scotch pies. Mayra had skipped breakfast, and now she'd have to bear a hollow middle until she returned home.

Pressing a hand against her rumbling tummy, she squared her shoulders. More than one unfortunate villager dealt with hunger daily these past months. Assuredly, she could endure another hour or so.

"G'day, Miss Findlay."

A ready grin split Reed MacPherson's winter-pale face when Horace nudged his chest, demanding the boy rub his withers.

As the lad reached for the reins before obliging the persistent horse, she smiled.

Standing on his toes, Reed scratched Horace's coat, just below his mane. "Ho, Horace. Ye like that, do ye?" Reed patted the gelding's side. "He's gettin' fatter, Miss."

"Indeed, he is. Which is why it takes me so long to make the journey, though it's barely three miles. He's a lazy laddie, he is." She adjusted her *bergère* hat—sadly in need of a fresh ribbon—to a slightly jauntier angle. But how could she justify a new embellishment when villagers went without necessities? "I'll only be a few moments, Reed—just long enough to give yer mum my apologies. My abigail ails, and I must see her swiftly home."

"Aye, miss. I'll keep 'im company for ye. Saved 'im a carrot, too."

Horace—his eyes half-closed in contentment—blew out a shuddery breath and bent his right leg. He'd not be pleased at having to turn right around and head for home. Too much exertion for one morning for the auld boy.

"Ye spoil him, Reed."

Giving a soft laugh, Mayra stood, and after pulling her wide skirt to the side, prepared to descend the cart, a task she usually managed well without assistance, despite wearing panniers.

Searc MacPherson exited the inn with a man she'd never seen before. Neck bent, Searc shook his head slowly at something the striking man said.

The stranger's arresting hazel eyes tangled with hers, jarring Mayra to her toes. And then he smiled—a dazzling flash of teeth in his tanned face.

In a twinkling, her mind went blank as a sheet of fresh foolscap.

In a completely foreign fashion, she became all gangly limbs, caught her toe on her hem, and with a strangled squawk—somewhere between a crane's whoop and a sheep's bleat—toppled right off the cart.

Into his arms.

Oh, curdled custard.

Leaping forward, somehow he'd managed to close the distance in a blink of an eye.

She found herself clasped to a marvelous, solidly muscled chest, while equally impressive firm arms cradled her shoulders and legs. The barest hint of mahogany whiskers shadowed the angular breadth of his neck and jaw—mere delicious inches away—and she forgot to breathe.

What a magnificent specimen of manhood. And he held her in his arms.

Quite the most spectacular accident ever to befall a maiden.

When her faulty lungs decided to function again, the most pleasant masculine scent filled her nostrils. Not a heavy fragrance, but a fresh, crisp, yet slightly musky scent—perhaps a hint of ale and tobacco, too.

She inhaled a thorough, prolonged breath. Probably indecorous, that, although neither Mum nor Bettie had ever specifically warned her against sniffing gentlemen.

Who was he?

Why hadn't she seen him in Glenliesh before?

Perhaps he only traveled through their unremarkable hamlet?

Och, of course he did. The small village offered little in the way of entertainment or commerce.

Why did the thought cause such profound disappointment?

Mayra wasn't free to harbor romantic notions; not

even in the most secret, most remote recesses of her mind. Well, fine, perhaps in the most clandestine, most isolated niches that even she daren't peek at except once or twice.

In the dark of night.

With her head buried beneath her thick coverlet.

From the *cuaran* boots enclosing the gentleman's feet to his nutmeg-colored jacket and dark blue waistcoat, the stranger's attire shouted quality. Hatless and tartan-free as he was, she couldn't hazard a guess as to his clan, or if he even boasted Scottish heritage at all.

Might he be a *Sassenach*?

A Frenchman?

Perhaps, but his vivid coloring implied Scots or Irish.

He cocked his russet head, and his eyes, an unusual but enthralling shade between summer moss and toasted almonds, glinted merrily at her. An unhurried smile bent his strong lips, revealing a charming dimple in his left cheek and further crimping the corner of his twinkling eyes. From the creases also framing his strong, still upturned mouth, it appeared he smiled habitually.

Instead of mortification engulfing her—as would be appropriate—of its own accord, her mouth swept upward, accompanied by a wave of sheer and wholly foreign giddiness.

And by rumbledethumps, she, Mayra Effie Lilias Findlay, was not the giddy, gay, flibbertigibbet sort.

Perfectly content, she made no effort to leave the blissful security of his arms, and he seemed disinclined to release her as well. And at five feet eight inches, she wasn't a wee sprite of a lass either. Yet his arms didn't tremble or shake with the exertion. In fact, she might've been a child, so effortlessly did he hold her.

Rather made her feel dainty and feminine.

And ever so naughty.

She peeked over his wide, sturdy shoulder.

Och and rot.

Bettie—Mum, as well—would cluck and fuss something awful, when they learned a man had held her—in public, too.

They would know soon enough, since a few

villagers had seen her ungraceful tumble, and even now stood gawking at the attractive stranger in their midst. The young ladies in particular seemed enthralled. They stared brazenly whilst striking provocative poses and thrusting their bosoms out, the whole while tittering about the *braw mon* with the wavy auburn hair.

How could Mayra blame them, when even though each scandalous moment she lingered in the '*braw mon's*' embrace heaped scoops of coal on the gossip fires, she couldn't bring herself to move an inch?

It wasn't every day a lass found herself in such a wonderfully awkward predicament.

Still, she ought to make some effort to leave his embrace.

Perhaps she'd contracted Bettie's ailment, and fever had addled her reason.

Mayra touched her cheek, aware his startling, amused greenish gaze trailed the movement.

Aye, verra warm.

That explained the languid heat encompassing her. Like warm honey trickled through her veins and turned her muscles to the consistency of hot-off-the-stove porridge.

And inarguably, no one had ever witnessed either warm honey or fresh porridge ever standing upright.

Finally clicking his gaping mouth closed, Searc trundled to her, his apron strings flapping against his ample behind. "Lass, I feared ye were about to take a nasty fall." He slapped the other man on his broad shoulder. "Good thing, Mr. Wallace's quicker on his feet than I am, aye?"

"Indeed. I'm most grateful." Must she sound so dafty and breathless? "Ye may put me down now, sir."

Or not.

I dinna mind stayin' in yer arms a trifle longer.

A week or so perhaps

As if he'd heard her, the handsome stranger's grasp firmed, pulling her minutely closer, his fingers pressing into the undersides of her thighs in a most thrilling way. A way that made her yearn to nestle closer, nuzzle his strong, delicious-smelling neck, and press her backside into his palms.

Another heady wave sluiced through her.

Was it her imagination, or did he seem almost as reluctant to release her as she was to have him set her down? After he lowered her to the ground, one of his hands lingered between her shoulder blades for a scrumptious, protracted moment. The heat penetrated her clothing, and she wouldn't be surprised when she disrobed tonight to find his palm imprinted on her back as if branded by his touch.

The urge to lean into his chest so overwhelmed her, she bit her lip.

What in highland heather had come over her?

She'd been too shielded from young, devilishly attractive men, that was what. Other than family members, no male had ever embraced her. Good thing, too, if this was her doaty reaction.

Except...

Mayra doubted she'd respond like this with just any mon.

A flush singed her already heated cheeks, and she set about righting her rumpled gown and lopsided hat, taking care to avoid the curious glances of the passersby. She must be above reproach, she well knew.

Hadn't that been drilled into her, over and over *and over* from the time she was a wee lass?

Aye, and Mayra always did what was expected of her.

Nonetheless, mightn't a scandal be just the thing to put her betrothed off?

Would her intended then *finally* grant her request to end their arrangement?

Perhaps.

As the idea took root, she paused with her fussing.

Aye, an innocent flirtation *was* just the thing.

Och, and when word reached—

"May I ken whom I've had the pleasure of rescuin'?" Her hero raked a big hand through his gingerish locks, ruffling the curls atop his head.

Ach. Bless Mayra's darned and mended stockings, Scots after all.

The way Mr. Wallace said pleasure, the word rolling from his tongue in a low, mesmerizing brogue-turned-purr, wrenched her attention from her ministrations to his much-too-enticing lips.

Since when did a man's mouth fascinate her so?

That same mouth notched up a trifle before her gaze inched higher to lock with his.

Her heart frolicked about behind her ribs like a litter of frisky kittens.

Guid help me.

A flirtation with this man might prove much too dangerous. Given her uncharacteristic, dazed response, *he* might be much too dangerous.

"Allow me to introduce ye." Searc beamed, his wide face wreathed in an enormous smile. "Miss Mayra Findlay, may I present Mr.— "

Searc scratched the back of his bulging neck, his face folded into confused creases. "I dinna recollect if ye told the missus yer first name when Mags registered ye."

Her hero dragged his attention from Mayra for an instant. "Och, aye... Coburn. Coburn Wallace."

As Mr. Wallace respectfully dipped his head, polite but not the least subservient, the sun caught the bronze streaks ribboning his russet hair.

"Mr. Coburn Wallace, Miss Mayra Findlay," Searc finished, another broad smile stretching his kind face, as if he'd been granted the highest honor in introducing them.

Mayra adjusted her sleeve, smoothing the slightly frayed cuff over her glove.

Ach. Not done.

Searc only meant to be helpful, but in introducing her to the stranger, he overstepped propriety. Mum and Bettie wouldn't be please.

Mayra ought to nod her head and sweep past the men without another word. Most peculiar thing, however. Her feet stayed fixed where Mr. Wallace had deposited her and seemed as loath to move as Glen Coe's majestic mountains towering beyond the horizon.

"Miss Findlay? Of Dunrangour Tower?"

A different glint, more keen and assessing rather than appreciative, entered Mr. Wallace's interesting eyes. His hot gaze leisurely crept to her scuffed half-boot clad feet, and then made the reverse journey over her well-worn midnight blue and hunter green arisaid to rest on her hair secured in a simple knot beneath her hat.

"Aye, I am." Mayra's stomach renewed its frolicking when he'd said her name. Mindful of the intrigued onlookers, she inclined her head in what she hoped was a regal, yet impersonal manner.

"May I ask what brings ye to our fair village, Mr. Wallace?"

2

Damn his eyes, Logan was in it to his raised brows now. And he detested trickery.

"I'm visitin' relatives after three years abroad, Miss Findlay."

Not exactly a lie, but enough of a deception that his conscience chafed worse than sliding across Loch Tolhorf's frozen surface.

Bare arsed.

More precisely, he'd left Lockelieth in outrage, after falling out with his father upon learning Da had spent a great deal—*nearly all, truth be told*—of Miss Findlay's dowry entrusted to his care until she and Logan wed.

Blinded by his much younger wife's exotic

beauty, Da had succumbed to Rodena's extravagant demands. In doing so, he'd forsworn his scruples, violated the settlement terms, and obligated Logan to honor the cursed troth.

Unless he paid back the monies. Monies he didn't possess.

That had spurred him to delve into a variety of risky business ventures while abroad, a few teetering on respectability's fringes, and none of which paid a quick return.

But then again, he'd believed he had at least another year to make his fortune before exchanging vows.

Only—*blast my damnable luck*—two months ago, he'd received word his father had fallen gravely ill. On the harried journey home, time and again Logan cursed himself for losing his temper and departing without telling Da farewell.

He'd arrived home mere days before his father died, leaving Logan an undisciplined clan, nigh on destitute serfs, a keep in deplorable condition, and empty estate coffers. Not to mention a widow more distraught about her future than her husband's death or the care of her young daughter, Isla.

For a fortnight after Da's death, Logan had prowled Lockelieth, half-pished in a grief-born fog, and later, a fury-born haze when he learned *all* of Mayra's dowry was now gone—squandered down to the last glistening pearl on Rodena.

And that wasn't the worst hell-fired news.

Da had secretly mortgaged Lockelieth to her glorious ramparts and parapets with an impossibly large payment due by year's end.

A payment Logan had no means of making.

At present, Mayra's lands—lands Da claimed contained valuable ores—and the rest of her dowry were all that stood between Lockelieth and financial ruin.

More importantly, and the compelling reason he couldn't cancel the union with Mayra Findlay, Logan's people had suffered neglect these past few years as Da poured all his resources into Rodena's grasping, talon-tipped fingers.

Logan's foreign business ventures had yet to

produce a significant profit, and his only recourse was to convince Mayra to marry him before her twentieth birthday.

Much sooner, truth to tell.

Ideally, as quickly as arrangements could be made.

No legal writ forbade him from wedding her sooner, just a reluctant six-year-old lad's oath of honor.

He eyed her, chatting with the boy petting her horse. She was as likely to agree to the rushed union as sheep were to frolic about wearing periwigs, sniffing snuff, and sipping sherry.

"Are ye from near here, Mr. Wallace?"

Mayra picked a piece of straw from her plaid. Her endearing, not so subtle, attempt to glean more information earned her an amused smile.

He'd piqued her interest.

Excellent.

Logan could almost see and hear her mind ticking off possibilities.

"I have family scattered hither and yon in Scotland

and England. Even a few in the New World, Miss Findlay."

True enough.

Unlike the falsehood he'd told her about his identity.

The lie spilled from his mouth before he could consider another, wiser, more honest option.

Coburn wouldn't be pleased when he learned of the ruse, and even less so when Logan asked him to keep his confidence regarding the matter. Coburn's integrity made even the most devout saint appear a black-hearted sinner.

Nevertheless, and despite Logan's lie relegating him to the worst sort of knave, he didn't want Mayra to know he was her affianced just yet. Particularly since a stack of letters requesting an end to their betrothal sat neatly within his desk's top drawer—an ever-present reminder of her disdain and reluctance.

That was one reason's he'd chosen to stay in the village for the time being, rather than venture to Dunrangour Tower directly. He was well within his rights to call on his intended, but he sought answers that he doubted he'd find at the keep.

After securing a room at The Dozing Stag for an undetermined length of time, Logan had exited the inn and spied a vision of such unexpected comeliness, his lungs stalled. And when his gaze collided with hers...

He knew.

Even before his attention locked on the Luckenbooth brooch, he *knew* she was Mayra Findlay—tall, fair, and blue-eyed like her sire, but with her mum's oval face, delicate bones, and bowed lips.

Never before had he experienced such a powerful and instant response to a woman.

And given her rosy cheeks and dazed expression, she'd been as awestruck.

Either that or she was a promiscuous piece, practiced at snaring men with her guise of false innocence.

He skewed his mouth sideways a fraction.

How jaded and pessimistic he'd become, all because Da had married a wanton, only to learn her true character too late.

For the briefest instant—not more than a heartbeat

really—Logan had almost told Mayra the truth. That this very day, *she* brought him to Glenliesh Village.

Or rather, seeking news of her had drawn him.

He'd opened his mouth to tell her, but unexpected and inexplicable fear of her reaction kept him mute.

What if her present fascination turned to contempt or scorn?

He still must wed her, willing or no', and he far preferred the former.

Instead, he'd held fast to his hastily-contrived plan: to poke around, and then contemplate his best course, depending on what he unearthed. He was fairly confident no one here would know of Coburn's kinship to him, so pretending to be his cousin shouldn't cause any issues.

Certainly, he didn't expect to encounter Mayra within an hour of arriving, nor could he have predicted his overwhelming reaction when he did. Even now, his jumbled thoughts caroused 'round in his mind, and his unruly member lay heavy and aching against his thigh.

Fine bloody time to don *Sassenach* garb.

A kilt would've saved him a great deal of

mortification, but someone was sure to have recognized the Rutherford cerulean and scarlet plaid. Bending his knee and angling his leg forward, he prayed Mayra didn't notice his arousal, as he unwisely permitted himself another languid perusal of her.

Enchanting didn't begin to describe Mayra.

Even the freckles dotting her upturned nose, her faintly lopsided smile, and a small scar over her right eyebrow charmed in a precocious, elfin way. And she possessed the most unusual voice. Uncommonly low and rich for a woman, her husky brogue wrapped around his senses, bewitching and ensnaring him.

What did her laugh sound like?

Her cries of passion?

Deep and sultry like her voice?

Gettin' miles ahead of yerself there, old chap.

Nevertheless, his manhood jerked in appreciation.

Damned intractable thing. Worse than an undisciplined pup.

Logan scrutinized her, trying to read her expression and gauge her thoughts.

No calculating or shrewdness shadowed Mayra's

clear blue gaze, and he relaxed the merest bit.

He'd stared into those wide eyes long ago, nearly two decades, before thick sable lashes framed them below winged, fawn-colored brows. His hungry gaze raked over her creamy skin, slightly turned up berry-pink mouth, dainty, yet strong chin, and her hair.

Och, what magnificent hair.

The bald bairn now boasted a glorious halo of moon-spun tendrils, partially hidden beneath an atrocious straw hat with the ugliest—*what was that ghastly color?*—ribbon he'd ever seen. Her arisaid's bright hues complimented her coloring, unlike the simple woolen gown of an indistinguishable shade somewhere between tree bark and muddy river bank brown.

She wasn't exactly attired in the first stare of fashion, yet she didn't seem ashamed or self-conscience of her clothing. Truthfully, he'd expected to find her wearing the finest English garments money could buy, as his stepmum was wont to do.

He angled his head and folded his arms.

That he recognized Mayra also flabbergasted him.

How many years since he'd last seen her?

Ten?

No, more.

The shy, awkward, rickle-a-bones lassie had blossomed into a rare and exquisite woman, and after holding that tempting armful scant moments before, he almost hurled his plans into the tosspot.

What difference did it make if she knew who he was now?

She would soon enough in any event.

Roderick Findlay's words—words Logan hadn't recalled until this moment—echoed in his head.

"Court her."

Why not?

He'd promised her father to woo her, hadn't he? A short courtship couldn't hurt, albeit he'd have to tell her who he was, and soon.

God's bones.

What if he succeeded in engaging her affections, and she fell in love with him?

The Coburn me?

Now that would be one hell of a conundrum.

No, he wouldn't let it go that far.

To do so would be unjust and cruel.

He'd given Lady Findlay his word he'd no hurt Mayra, and Logan was a man of his word. Even if the oath had been given as a wee, confused lad who'd only coveted another sword fight with his cousin before he had to endure a tedious coach ride home.

A self-recriminating smile pulled Logan's mouth sideways once more.

Hadn't he also vowed—quite adamantly, as he recalled—he never wanted to touch Mayra?

Ever.

And he'd also promised to try to love her.

That sentiment had come full circle, and after embracing her lush form, he itched to touch—taste, caress, and kiss, too—every last inch of her pearly skin, to run his fingers through her marvelous silky mane of hair, and sample her mouth that looked to have just eaten ripe raspberries.

Could those lips possibly taste as sweet as they appeared or her hair feel as soft as the glossy cloud atop her head promised?

Primal male satisfaction thrummed through him.

By Hades, she was already his.

His!

Until this moment, he'd refused to admit the fact or, for that matter, acknowledge the distasteful, unwanted betrothal at all. Years ago, he'd managed to stuff the inconvenience into a grim corner of his mind and live his life as he pleased, more or less.

The awareness that he should've asked to have the agreement voided niggled the tattered edges of his conscience every now and again, and he'd always dismissed the task as an inconvenience he'd attend to later.

Except—*devil seize it*—he'd waited too damned long to petition the Crown.

And now...

A familiar tremor of frustrated anger prodded his gut.

Now, thanks to Da and that vain hellcat he married, Logan was stuck faster than an ant in cement.

Marry Mayra Findlay he would, regardless of where her affections or interests might lie.

He'd no choice, but he'd garner her true character beforehand and take precautions as needed if she proved to be something other than a virtuous woman.

Pointedly redirecting his melancholic musings, Logan turned his attention to the purpose of his visit—to learn as much as he could about his luscious intended.

"How, if I may be so bold as to ask, do ye ken of me?" Mayra's patient, expectant gaze held his.

No timid, retiring miss here, but neither, he'd vow, was she a flirt.

Aye, but appearances could be mightily deceptive, as he and Da—God rest his sorry soul—could attest.

Rodena's beautiful, haughty face popped to mind, souring Logan's jovial mood again.

He'd not be cuckolded and humiliated—forced to acknowledge another man's seed as his offspring as Da had been.

Stupid, besotted auld fool, falling under Rodena's spell.

In the end, her sluttish behavior, avariciousness, and cold, callous disregard strangled Da's affection and crushed his heart. No surprise he'd died of heart failure.

Suddenly weary, Logan passed a hand over his eyes.

Enough ruminating about that banshee when an angel stood before him.

Innocent interest filled Mayra's frank yet intelligent gaze, the color of the Highland's early morning summer sky.

He didn't detect a trace of coquetry or seduction, and he found her lack of guile all the more appealing. His betrothed wasn't a wanton, nor did she seem spoiled, as many pampered, high-born daughters were.

How to answer Mayra's question?

How *had* he heard of her?

She'd not be hearing the truth, just yet.

He wasn't an idiot. He couldn't afford to frighten her off.

Precisely how peeved would she be when he told her who he really was?

He'd encountered her but five minutes ago, yet he'd wager her remaining dowry—the half the

Findlays still held—she wasn't the type to overlook deceit, which made his situation all the more precarious.

Although he didn't want to take an infuriated lass to wife, he must uncover what prompted her zealous and repeated—two-and-twenty at last count—requests to terminate their agreement.

To be fair, Mayra hadn't had any more say in the arrangement than Logan. But since he couldn't grant her plea and free her, he'd do his utmost to court her.

He wasn't foolish enough to suppose he might easily win her heart.

Her letters, polite and straightforward, clearly indicated she thought him a negligent, selfish, boorish jackanapes.

In a bothersome very brief time he'd have to prove he wasn't.

But what about this mammoth lie?

Fine, prove he wasn't a complete and utter blackguard then.

Slamming the door on his musings, he gave her his most disarming smile.

She blinked as if momentarily stunned. Or was she unaccustomed to male attention?

Now that presented an interesting scenario.

"I seem to remember someone mentionin' ye in connection with Dunrangour when I was in Edinburgh last month, Miss Findlay."

He scrambled to summon the name of an acquaintance they might have in common, but someone she wasn't intimate with if she asked who.

Instead of inquiring, however, her pretty mouth turned upward a trifle.

"My dearest friend, Gaira Windlespoon is to wed there in April. And my mum is accompanying me to the city for the ceremony. There's to be a masque ball. I've never attended a ball either."

Didn't the Findlays not entertain, then?

Melancholy and yearning colored her throaty voice. "I've heard it's a lovely city, and I've always wondered how different life is there from the Highlands."

"Edinburgh has many stunnin' features to be sure, but as with all highly-populated places, poverty and sanitation issues abounded. I dinna mind visitin', but I'd never want to live there."

After three years, Logan was good and done with urban life, particularly filthy, malodorous port cities. Mayra couldn't imagine town squalor, the stench, or the impoverishment if she'd never seen or smelled them.

Fair brow furrowed in faint, but noticeable lines, she swept the village a wistful glance.

"We've privation here as well, Mr. Wallace. In fact, that's why I came to town. To deliver food baskets. But now, I really must be off. My maid awaits me, and I've duties to attend to at home."

Times were tough for many, and word had it the Dunrangour didn't fare that much better than Lockelieth since laird Roderick Findlay's death two years ago. That explained Mayra's humble attire, and yet she provided food to hungry villagers.

Had the Findlays been forced to tap into her remaining dowry? Perhaps that was why she was so insistent upon ending their betrothal.

What would happen to Lockelieth then?

What would happen to Mayra?

Dowerless, she wasn't likely to find another respectable offer.

Ach, but she wasn't entirely dowerless, was she?

The land settled upon her was quite valuable. Particularly if it contained copper and silver, as rumored.

A peely-wally sensation churned his gut.

It mattered not.

He couldn't release her.

Not without returning the other portion. The squandered share.

His honor wouldn't permit anything less, and aside from selling Lockelieth's acres, he had no way of doing so, and without land, the estate couldn't support itself.

Bloody fine situation his father had left Logan to sort out.

Mayra gave MacPherson, intently watching their exchange, a cheery smile.

"Would ye please give yer wife my apologies? Bettie ails, and I must fetch her and see her home. Tell

Maggi I promise to have tea when I return on Friday."

"Aye, lass. She'll be disappointed, I've nae doubt, but ye're wise to see Bettie to the keep. I'll tell my missus fer ye now." He extended his palm to Logan, and the men shook hands. "It's welcome ye be to stay for as long as ye like, sir."

After shaking hands, he gestured to the skinny boy tending Mayra's horse. "As soon as Miss Findlay leaves, Reed, git yerself to the stables and help yer brother finish muckin' the stalls. Then both of ye come in and eat."

"Aye, Da." Reed shook his head, his overly-long shock of sandy hair flying about his neck as he rubbed the dozing horse's forehead.

With a polite, deferential dip of his head, MacPherson sauntered back into the inn.

Logan patted the boy's shoulder. "Ye go along, lad. I can assist Miss Findlay. I can hear yer stomach rumblin' from here."

"Thank ye, sir!" Reed bobbed his tousled head, giving them a gap-toothed grin. "Until Friday, Miss."

He tore to the stables, his scrawny legs churning.

Mayra's charming smile and the pink tinging her satiny cheeks suggested she wasn't opposed to Logan's assistance. Or else he'd quite forgotten how to read a woman's interest, and he hadn't been celibate *that* long, by God.

Taking her elbow, Logan guided her the few feet back to the cart.

"It was a pleasure to make yer acquaintance, Miss Findlay. I pray I might have the honor of seein' ye again."

3

Wicked of Logan to suggest it. To test Mayra.
Without giving her any notion of his status or standing.

He couldn't decide which he wanted more—for her to politely defer and say she couldn't, or to eagerly agree.

Hesitation shadowing her features, as if she weren't certain how to respond, she brushed a stray strand of silky, flaxen hair behind her ear. Indecision warred with desire in her lovely eyes. She sensed the immediate attraction too, but if she were the innocent he hoped, unlike him, she wasn't sure precisely what she felt.

Mayra gazed at him with such intensity—

innocence mixed with keen interest and perhaps more than a little uncertainty.

She doesn't ken who ye really are.

She would. And soon.

After all, he didn't have time to dawdle in an extended courtship. A month—two at most. For the time being, he'd pursue and enjoy this peculiar enchantment.

He well knew he might not like what he uncovered about Mayra Findlay, but he knew his duty too.

"May I help ye?" He canted his head toward the cart's seat, while gesturing.

She searched his face and something deep within her eyes mellowed.

"Aye. Please."

In one adroit movement, Logan placed his hands around her trim waist and hoisted her onto the cart. His palms continued to tingle, wrist to fingertips, from the completely chaste contact.

"Thank ye, Mr. Wallace. I should like for us to meet again."

What would she propose?

Once settled on the seat, she accepted the reins he extended.

"I come to the village twice a week. Tuesday and Friday mornings, and I generally take tea at the inn with Mrs. MacPherson when I do."

Clever lass. She hadn't committed to seeing him, but she'd let him know her interest, all the while staying inside propriety's boundaries.

"I shall eagerly anticipate Friday's arrival then."

Giving him her fetching, slightly off-center smile, she clicked her tongue. "Walk on, Horace."

The portly gelding reluctantly ambled forward, and hands on his hips, Logan didn't move until the cart rattled around a corner.

Look back.

Just before Mayra disappeared, she cast a furtive glance over her shoulder, and he waved once.

Her lips tilted, but she didn't return the gesture.

Swinging to face the inn, he bumped into a passing matron.

Hell's bells and cockle shells.

"Logan, lad? Be that really ye?"

Two days later, the tension bunching Logan's shoulders eased as the drizzly dawn's pewter gray revealed a figure lounging, one knee raised, on a boulder beside Loch Tolhorf.

A horse grazed nearby, and fog drifted lazily upward from the ebony waters, shrouding all but the topmost limbs of the pines dotting the far shoreline.

Coburn had received Logan's message.

At his approach, his cousin turned his head and pulled his tam lower over his ears, but didn't bother rising.

"Pray tell me what was so urgent I had to freeze my ballocks aff waitin' for ye in the dark at this ungodly hour, Logan? I had to ride most of the night to make it here on time."

A tiny vapor cloud accompanied each peeved, weary word. Coburn didn't like to be separated from his mattress, or whatever lass had warmed his bed, before the sun rose.

A grin threatened, but Logan wrestled it into submission. He needed his cousin's cooperation. Must have it, else his plan would evaporate as surely as the thick mist now hovering between the trees' trunks.

"I want to assure ye stay away from Glenliesh while I'm there." He absently stroked his mount's neck. "Actually, it might be better if ye left the area altogether for a while. Mayhap a trip to Edinburgh?"

He offered a cheery smile to offset his blunt suggestion.

Jacca, Logan's smoky cream gelding, snorted and stamped his feet, and Coburn adjusted his collar higher to block the bone-piercing breeze.

Aye, wretchedly brisk this morning.

Even with coat and plaid, frigid little toes scampered the length of Logan's spine, and a shudder shook him.

The cold dampness crept into the creases and crannies, and settled heavy and dank in a person's marrow, reluctant to leave even when one went indoors.

"And why, exactly, would I want to do any such thin', cousin?" Coburn arched a smug brow.

Logan scratched his temple, tempering what he had to say with a hitched shoulder and a deliberate nonchalant mien. Coburn wasn't going to be pleased.

"I may have led the villagers and my betrothed to think that I'm ye."

His heart had dived to his boots and squirmed there, like weevils in porridge oats, several uncomfortable moments when he'd bumped into Lockelieth's former cook the other day.

How could he possibly have forgotten Annag Homles lived with her daughter in Glenliesh now? She might very well ruin his hastily contrived scheme.

Annag had promised to keep his secret, but unease nipped sharply, nonetheless.

As a child he'd heard her blethering with the other servants, though never maliciously. He prayed loyalty would seal her lips. At least long enough to win Mayra's favor.

"May have? By chance? In passin'?" Coburn

lurched to his feet, his eyes flint hard and angry as he glared at Logan. "Are ye aff yer bloody heid?"

"Nae." *Not completely, anyway.* "I'm just a fool who acted impulsively and didna control his tongue." Logan dismounted and explained his encounter with Mayra, leaving off his immediate, profound attraction and fascination.

His cousin wouldn't be able to resist roasting him. As it was suspicion danced in his astute gaze.

"I want to discover why she's so desperate to end our betrothal, and after what Rodena did to Da, I dinna want any foul surprises when we're married."

Fishing around in his coat pocket, Coburn grumbled, "Ye're a damned, stupid imbecile. And what's more, it's no' like ye at all. In fact, ye despise charlatans and frauds. Anythin' remotely disreputable and ye distance yerself."

Everything Coburn said was usually true.

Coburn shook his head, puzzlement folding his brow. "Ye ken she'll be furious when ye tell her? And ye'd better hope to Guid she doesn't uncover the truth on her own."

"I've considered that possibility," Logan admitted. "Which is why I asked ye to meet me here at this miserable hour."

Mouth pressed into a bitter line, Coburn shook his head. "Bloody glad I am that I'm no' ye."

"So ye've mentioned several times previously." Irony, dryer than burnt toast, leeched into Logan's voice. His cousin had never envied Login's position, finding the responsibility and duties too demanding and constraining. "I promise ye, if ye met her ye'd think much differently."

"*Aahhh.*"

Coburn dragged the word out, his eyes fairly dancing with gloating amusement, his mouth quirked into a damned annoying grin. "So it's like that, is it? She's grown into a beauty." He jabbed a finger toward Logan's chest. "And ye're itchin' to bed the lass. Explains a lot. Aye, it does indeed."

Logan donned a battle-scarred glower but choked off his immediate vulgar retort.

He found Mayra's keen wit every bit as attractive as her face and form—*well almost*—but he'd forsake whisky for a month before admitting any such thing to Coburn.

"I dinna ken if'n I want to make myself scarce." Rubbing his chin, Coburn tilted his head. "Maybe I want to see this lass that's caused ye to hurl aside yer common sense and act the moon-eyed swain."

"Go bugger yerself, cousin." So much for controlling his temper.

Coburn's shout of laughter startled a large bird from its nest. The annoyed *ke-ke*, identified a goshawk taking wing.

"Nae need. I have lasses standin' in line to warm my bed. And unlike ye, I occasionally—"*more often than not, cousin*—"take advantage of their generous offers."

"Since I have nae desire to hear about yer latest romantic exploit, I'll be on my way. Mayra leaves for Edinburgh shortly. I'll send word when she does. Wouldn't do for her to encounter ye there, though—even if I have told her the whole of it by then." Logan raised a commanding brow. The one that told his cousin to hold his wheesht. Or else. "If I'm successful, we may have a wedding date set by then, too."

That didn't give him long to accomplish what he needed to. Mayra's twice-weekly trips to Glenliesh would have to suffice unless he found other opportunities to spend time with her.

But not at Dunrangour Tower, while he still pretended to be Coburn Wallace.

Lady Findlay most definitely wouldn't approve or permit such outrageousness.

"Just a moment." Coburn finally withdrew a crumpled letter then proceeded to try to smooth the deep creases. Extending the hopelessly wrinkled missive, he wiggled the paper, which crackled and rattled in protest.

"This came for ye yesterday. It's from yer Miss Findlay."

"Nae doubt another appeal to terminate our agreement."

Accepting the note, Logan grimaced, and after quickly glancing at her neat, feminine script, tucked the rectangle into his jacket. He wasn't about to read it with his grinning-like-an-imbecile-cousin looking on.

He patted his chest. "I believe this makes three-and-twenty. She's persistent. I'll give her that."

Persistent. Intriguing. Beguiling.

Not what he expected at all. Although what he had anticipated, he couldn't quite define. His thoughts marching along those sentimental paths might prove worrisome, however.

Coburn angled his coppery head, his astute gaze probing. "And after ye've finished pokin' about, do ye intend to cry off if'n ye uncover somethin' ... ah ... untoward or unpleasant?"

If only Logan could have done so.

Heaving a gusty breath, he gave the merest negative shake of his head. "Nae, I cannae. Ye ken Da spent part of the dowry, and I have nae way to repay it."

"Aye. I ken, Logan. But if'n ye're still keen on weddin' and beddin' the lass, why skulk around?"

Logan studied the Scots pines' angular forms ringing the loch's other side, where a rare, brave moonbeam slashed the fog and tickled the water's glistening surface.

"Just a few more minutes, boy," Coburn patted his restless mount's withers.

Devil it.

Logan was loath to admit the ugly truth, even to the person he held dearest. Though he was obligated to marry Mayra, if she turned out to be a wanton harlot, he could at least refrain from giving her his heart, no matter how enticing her lips, mesmerizing her eyes, or alluring the rest of her luscious form.

"Well, Logan? I have a right to ken why ye're impersonatin' me. Particularly since my decorum, charm, taste in clothin', and appeal to the fairer sex far exceeds yers." Coburn gave him a rakish wink.

His cousin baited him, but Logan refused to take the lure.

"I'd like to ken what I'm getting beforehand," Logan said, matter of fact. "I winna be made a fool, an object of scorn and pity, like Da."

Head tilted, Coburn regarded Logan for an extended, contemplative moment.

"Fine. Ye can pretend to be me. And I'll keep my distance." Coburn's derisive smile revealed his grudging acquiescence. "But my advice, *my preference*, is that ye tell Miss Findlay the truth. And sooner, rather than later. Deception's always a two-edged sword. And mark my words, Cousin, ye'll bitterly regret this sham."

A jot more tension dissolved, easing the tautness squeezing Logan's ribs.

He could always count on Coburn to have his back.

"Mayra's attending a wedding in Edinburgh in April, and I hope to put things right long before then," he said, eyeing a red stag lurking at the forest's edge.

"Speakin' of Edinburgh," Coburn gathered his horse's reins, "Rodena took Isla and trundled off to her sister's there. A Lady Featherstone? Featherspoon? *Featherbrain?* Lady Feather Somebody-or-other, she claimed."

Good riddance.

Logan had wanted to send her packing for weeks, and only Isla prevented him from doing so.

"Did my stepmum abscond with the silver and anythin' else of worth she could steal?"

"Nae." Coburn shook his head and gave the cranky sky an equally cantankerous frown. "I had the servants watch her every move. She screeched and swore like a *hoore,* but in the end, she only took their clothin' and personal effects. Most wise of ye to lock the family jewels in the safe."

"Honestly, I expected all of the more valuable pieces to have been sold long ago. I suppose I owe that small reprieve to Rodena's greed and lust for glittery baubles." Logan rewrapped the wool scarf circling his neck.

Damned fickle weather. Worse than a popular courtesan.

"The poor, wee lass sobbed uncontrollably. She didna want to leave Lockelieth. Or ye." Coburn patted his restless stallion again.

Rodena ought to have left Isla at Lockelieth. The child would've been better off away from her sluttish mum.

Coburn swung into the saddle. "I haven't been to Edinburgh in over a month. I'll go to town and see what mischief yer promiscuous stepmum embroils herself in. I'll admit to feelin' sorry for Isla. She's a sweet thing. Do ye ken yet who sired her?"

"Nae, and I doubt Rodena does either."

Logan scowled, relief that his stepmum had departed, but pity for her child nudging his conscience. "Whilst ye're in town, would ye mind doin' a bit of research about silver and copper minin' in this region? Supposedly, there's a lode on the dowered parcel of Dunrangour's land. I'd like to ken if there's any basis to the rumor."

"Wouldn't the locals be more likely to ken that?" Coburn scratched a bold eyebrow as another disgruntled bird took wing.

Logan inclined his head. "Possibly, but I'm guessin' official records would be kept in Edinburgh."

"Aye, I shall poke around." Coburn pressed his lips together, his countenance gone serious and stern. "Logan, dinna wait too long to tell Miss Findlay. A marriage begun with distrust and deceit likely winna improve in time."

Since when was his rakehell cousin an authority on the fairer sex?

Logan offered a twisted grin. "I ken ye're right. But I'm calf-deep in shite now. Nae help but to wade through it."

He, too, climbed into the saddle. "Coburn?"

Already picking his way along the rocky terrain, his cousin glanced up. "Aye?"

"Thank ye."

Coburn jostled his shoulders. "Ye're all I have left for kin, and I dinna want ye unhappy. Ye're an insufferable grouch when ye are." Affection crinkled the planes of his face and thickened his brogue.

"Send word if ye need me, cousin, and I'll keep ye appraised of yer stepmum's activities."

4

Mayra cast an anxious eye to the sullen, armor-tinted sky and held the dogcart's reins with one hand while pulling her arisaid over her head with the other. She absently checked to assure the brooch securing the plaid rested in its designated place above her breasts.

"Get on with ye, Horace." She clicked her tongue.

The obstinate gelding flicked his ears back, but ignored her prompting and continued his unhurried plodding.

By crackers, she'd have made better time astride a ram.

Sidesaddle.

"Come on. Go it!" She changed her tone to cajoling. "I'll give ye an extra portion of oats if'n ye pick up yer pace, sweet laddie. An apple, too."

Maybe speaking to him in Scots would work.

Horace lazily glanced over his tawny shoulder, a distinct superior glint in his soft brandy-brown eyes, and barred his yellow teeth—*does he dare mock me?*—before facing forward and continuing his same sluggish gait.

A black slug *did* trot along swifter.

"Och, ye ... ye stubborn, dafty ... mule."

No ruder insult could she have hurled upon the gentle beast's head. She loved him, but he could be so very obstinate. And today of all days she was in a terrible rush. For reasons other than the belligerent weather too.

The day after tomorrow she departed for Edinburgh, and she didn't know when she'd see Coburn again. Chances were, he'd not still be in the village when they returned at the end of April.

At the unwelcome truth, heaviness settled in her middle.

This was her fourth trip to the village since meeting him, and each prior time she'd encountered

Coburn, he'd given her a sigh-worthy smile, warm and inviting, as if he were as happy to see her as she was him.

And when he trailed his gaze over her, Mayra's flesh reacted in the most remarkable way—at once tingly and prickly, but also languid and melty.

She tipped her mouth sideways.

Was melty even a word?

Seated in The Dozing Stag's common room, like old friends, she and Coburn had chatted about all manner of polite, mundane things. She'd nibbled shortbread and sipped Maggi's special blend of tea, while he savored a warm ale.

Her brothers, Bhric and Monroe, eager to visit village friends, left her to herself, either unaware of her rendezvous with Coburn, or deeming them harmless in a public room.

When the time came to depart for home—always far too soon—Coburn had asked to walk Mayra to the village's edge, despite her brothers' certain curious gazes and mocking grins.

She'd wanted to agree, but nonetheless, prudence

dictated she decline his offer.

The lads would surely tell Mum, and that would be the end of any further outings.

Still, as faithful Horace had moseyed home, and her brothers good-naturedly ribbed one another or sang risqué ditties, she'd dared harbor secret thoughts.

Hopeful, fanciful, impossible thoughts.

And today, she'd see Coburn again.

She sighed, her mouth curved into a private smile.

Her heart raced and her tummy quivered in anticipation. No, downright, well...giddiness.

Mayra hoped—oh, how she hoped!—providence favored her today.

A dreamy smile bent her mouth once more.

She'd never met anyone—more specifically, any toe-curling, nape-raising, stomach-tumbling *mon*— quite like him.

A charmer who, in an instant, made such a lasting and pulse-stuttering impression; she could yet recall his brilliant smile and his hands on her person. Never mind his intelligent, sable-lashed, mossy-green eyes, chestnut hair, glinting deep bronze where the sun caressed it, or his angular face—high cheekbones, chiseled chin, noble forehead.

His deep, lyrical voice, like melted chocolate—sweet and warm—mesmerized her from the instant she heard him laugh at something MacPherson said as they exited the inn.

In her mind, he'd become an incomparable.

Another fretful survey of the irritable heavens, and Mayra puffed out her cheeks in frustration. Sure as chickens clucked, the portly, vicious-looking clouds were about to burst, and she'd be a sopped wretch by the time she made Glenliesh—guaranteeing her visit and the trip home would be utterly miserable.

And such unusual pains she'd taken with her appearance today, too.

She wore one of her best gowns—a stretch, calling the three-year old green-and-white striped garment such. She'd even dabbed a drop of her precious perfume behind each ear—her last gift from Da before he died.

Reaching beneath the soft plaid draped across her head, she patted her hair, then checked the pins and curls. Everything still felt in place. This new style—one which Gaira insisted was all the rage in Paris and London—seemed rather more trouble than it was worth.

And, truth be told, appeared much more bird nest-like than a fashionable coiffeure.

Mayra had spent hours on her toilette this morning, hence her delay in leaving the keep until afternoon. She feared moving her head too fast lest the whole tangle tumble loose and plop onto her shoulders.

If her head became wet, the carefully-arranged locks would droop faster than flower stems jammed into hot tea. She'd toddle into the village resembling one of the scruffy, highland cattle contentedly chewing their cud in the adjacent field.

A sudden gust whisked past, ruffling the cattle's coats, and Mayra clapped her hand atop her head to hold the arisaid in place.

Perfectly lovely.

A cow lifted her head and peered at Mayra through the wavy veil covering her broad forehead. The beast's pink tongue slid out, and she licked her nose.

Another stiff breeze blew past, and a shiver pelted down the column of Mayra's spine faster than a mouse dashing to its hidey-hole. She shuddered again, and drew her plaid tighter around her shoulders.

Vanity had her freezing her bum off.

Och, for certain she wouldn't mind having the cattle's thick, rain-repellent coats right now.

In the distance, the grouchy chain mail-hued sky grumbled as thunderclouds billowed across the temperamental firmament. From the corner of her eye, she glimpsed a sudden blue flash.

Lightening too?

Why must the weather be so confounded uncooperative today?

Despite the bitter weather, her spirit remained optimistic, for she made the trip to the village alone, and the new independence was glorious.

Only yesterday had Bettie finally felt well enough to leave her bed, so having her accompany Mayra today was out of the question. The boys—bless them for being mischievous whelps—were confined to their rooms for hiding their tutor's clothing.

Every last stitch.

And right before they were to depart the keep, Mum developed one of her wicked megrims. After taking headache powders and a hefty dose of laudanum, she'd taken to her bed.

Which meant—*joy of joys!*—after a great deal of finagling and convincing Mum that the poor, hungry souls in Glenliesh expected Mayra today, she bounced along on the dog cart by herself.

Not a grand escapade, but she'd cherish it nevertheless. She'd be perfectly safe on the short excursion without a clansman along to shadow her every move.

Sometimes, Mayra simply needed time alone. Needed to try new things; needed an adventure—to experience more of life outside Dunrangour Tower's massive walls.

Especially...

Heaving an audible sigh, she adjusted the reins, giving Horace more slack.

Especially if, despite all her attempts to the

contrary, she wound up mistress of Lockelieth after all.

In just over a year

One oh-so-wretchedly-short year.

She slumped on the padded seat until her stays pinched and forced her to sit upright again.

Nothing like ruminating about her neglectful intended, Logan Rutherford, to make a gloomy day even drearier. *That* albatross had hung round her neck since the first time a village boy winked at her, and she blushed and giggled with youthful pleasure.

Mum had wrapped an arm about Mayra's thin shoulders and gently explained she was betrothed and even at seven years old, she mustn't smile at or flirt with boys.

How does a wee lass flirt?

For that matter, how does an adult lass?

Did she dare try her hand today?

It couldn't be that difficult, could it?

No, but she'd not make a fool of herself, batting her lashes and puffing out her bosoms, all the while smiling coyly, as the village lasses had done that first day as they'd ogled Coburn.

Surely there were more subtle, less forward means of showing a gentleman he intrigued her.

In almost nineteen years, Mayra had no experience in the art. Shielded from male attention and company, almost as if her parents feared she'd bring ruin upon herself, and therefore them, she confessed to a shy awkwardness around men.

But she was betrothed, and therefore she needn't acquire the skill.

If Da hadn't stipulated she wait until her twentieth birthday to wed, she might already call Lockelieth Keep home and Rutherford her husband.

Utterly appalling.

Glee and excitement didn't cause her capering stomach's rolling this time, or the shudder rippling from shoulder to waist, like dragon's giant, razor-tipped claws scraping her spine.

How many times had she begged her parents to end the troth?

However, until her strapping Da died from pneumonia, of all things, they'd adamantly maintained Rutherford must be the one to seek King George's permission to terminate the contract. And—curse him for being an uncaring, selfish cull—Logan Rutherford remained exasperatingly, annoyingly, infuriatingly silent on the matter.

Bah.

Why, for all the oats in Scotland, didn't he respond to their letters?

King William died six months after he'd insisted on the match between them. Surely King George would grant Rutherford's request if the obstinate man would only ask.

And toward that end, Mayra had brazenly sent off another missive asking not only that Rutherford do so at his earliest convenience, but she'd also sent an epistle to King George, ever-so-politely requesting His Majesty to consider voiding the contract as well.

What harm could come of it?

If the king denied her appeal, at least she'd have tried everything at her disposal, short of gamboling off to the colonies.

Chin tucked to her chest to block the stinging wind, she gave an impish chuckle.

Horace flicked his ears and half turned his head.

"I'm nae laughin' at ye. Just my foppish intended."

Wouldn't she have liked to see Logan Rutherford's arrogant face when he read that last part of her letter? Probably sent the popinjay into a conniption.

She may have also hinted to Rutherford that she'd prefer to wed someone who actually showed an interest in her.

A *mon* who wasn't just taken with her dowry and land—a dowry that would've gone far to help support Dunrangour had Da permitted them to touch it.

He'd refused, saying Findlay honor forbade it.

Still, she'd prefer a *mon* she could love. One who demonstrated common courtesy—for instance, answering letters or preventing lasses from potentially nasty tumbles.

A particular dashing auburn-haired highlander with a rogue's smile and a rakish glint in his captivating eyes?

Eyes that one moment glowed like warm, dark

honey edged with forest green, and the next, the browns and greens spiraled together. But eyes that always danced with a faintly seductive glint around the edges.

What color were Rutherford's eyes?

Squinting at Horace's wide, swaying behind, Mayra tried to recall.

Blue? Brown?

Devil red?

She hadn't seen him since she was seven, and all she recalled from that painful encounter as she peeked from behind Mum's skirts, was dark coppery hair above a benign, albeit bored countenance.

Mayra drew in a cleansing breath.

No sense stewing on her betrothal unpleasantness right now, for she fully intended to make the most of every single moment of freedom she had left.

If the king and Rutherford proved uncooperative.

Heaven help her if they did.

She wriggled the reins the teeniest bit.

"Come on, Horace. Please. I cannae arrive looking like a selkie. No' today." Leaning forward a few inches, she confessed to the horse's broad back. "Coburn might be in the village again."

He simply must be.

Wicked of her to entertain such thoughts, but fanciful imaginations weren't actions. She knew her current status made her ineligible, but conversation was harmless, was it not? And she did so want to further her acquaintance with him even if naught could come of it.

Nothing outrageous or reproachful—

Wait a devilish moment...

She'd harbored this thought before, too.

Why, a scandal might be just the thing to make Logan Rutherford call off the betrothal.

Mum had emphasized over and over—*and over*— that he loathed any hint of impropriety.

Eyes slightly narrowed, her mind churning, Myra contemplated the feasibility.

Aye, it just might work.

Of course, she'd have to be cunning and cautious.

Verra, verra careful.

Her goal wasn't ruination, but simply to rid herself

of an unwanted intended.

Still, her interest in Coburn was real. Disturbingly so. She'd best be vigilant in that regard, too. He might prove to be a rapscallion or rake. A knave or reprobate, despite his overwhelming charm.

Mum and Bettie avowed men of that ilk were the hardest to trust, and a prudent woman wouldn't be so unwise. But how might Mayra discern the truth? She had pitiful, limited experience with men, and she couldn't exactly ask anyone outright.

Pardon me, but can ye tell me what ye ken of debonair Mr. Coburn Wallace?

Is he a womanizer, tippler, or given to gambling?

That would surely arch knowing, judgmental brows and send tongues to flapping faster than leaves during a spring storm, much like the one that threatened today. And of course it had to be during the only trip in weeks where no pressing errands demanded Mayra's attention.

Except for the usual food deliveries and collecting a new length of ribbon for her hat, she was free to do what she wished for the afternoon. Mum insisted on the new hat trim, claiming Mayra was soon to be Lady Rutherford, and she couldn't go about looking beggarly.

If beggarly put off Logan Rutherford, Mayra would take to wearing her oldest gown and shoes. No, she'd go about barefoot with dirt between her toes.

Wasn't there a frayed cap in the rag bag? And a moth-eaten shawl too?

Mayhap, she'd even smear a bit of earth or ashes on her chin and beneath her nails.

A grin split her face until Mum's and Bettie's horrified expressions intruded upon her humorous imaginings. They'd have apoplexy if she ambled about with a smudged face and soiled hands. Hard enough to explain wearing rags without having to justify a grimy countenance.

Nevertheless, the idea had merit.

A blustery gust slammed into her, and Horace's swishing tail indicated he found the weather as objectionable as she. A downpour would have him in a full-on sulk, and he might very well decline to tramp home.

It wouldn't be the first time the pigheaded beast refused to move his plump posterior, which is why he was one of the few remaining horses at Dunrangour.

Mayra quite anticipated a cup of steaming tea, a cozy midday meal, and a long visit with Maggi MacPherson. She might spare an entire two, or even three hours in the village if Coburn put in his usual appearance.

Everything depended on the feckless weather, of course.

The air had gradually grown thicker and damper, and the sky had developed a peculiar greenish cast, as the increasing wind tormented everything within its path.

Shivering, Mayra entreated Horace once more, appealing to the horse's preference for comfort.

"Ye do ken ye'll get soaked, and ye'll remain cold and wet 'til we get home?"

If they made it back to the keep this afternoon.

What she'd thought to be a typical bout of foul March weather looked to have developed into something much more serious.

To her delight, as if he understood he'd be subjected to a degree of discomfort, Horace broke into a slow trot.

Five minutes later, the heavens having been merciful and refraining from dumping their contents on the already soggy Highlands, she tooled the vehicle along the village's main street. Upon spying a broad-shouldered, bronze-haired man striding into the lodging house, her heart beat faster, and she gave a tiny whoop of excitement.

Coburn.

5

Logan entered The Dozing Stag, sorely tempted to seek his chamber and indulge in a long nap. After another sleepless night and rising before dawn again today, sand scraped across his eyes each time he blinked his millstone-weighted eyelids.

Later returning to the village than he'd intended, his hours exploring the acreage Findlay dowered Mayra had proved most satisfying. Logan had found prime grazing lands, as well as several acres suitable for crops. A rocky crag, tunneling along the property's northern perimeter separating the dowered lands from the rest of Dunrangour's, needed further exploring, too.

Da swore that piece contained copper and silver

ores, though he never revealed how he'd come by the information.

Logan blinked drowsily, the movement sluggish and forced as he plowed his fingers through his thick hair in an effort to calm the wind-blown strands.

Head wooly from lack of sleep, he inclined his head at the smattering of patrons gawking to see who entered on such a blustery afternoon. A yawn escaped him as he scanned the common room.

No striking lass with moonlight gleaming in her silken hair, peaches tinting her cheeks or summer's sky reflected in her winsome eyes, sipped tea and nibbled shortbread.

By Odin, Mayra even had his musings waxing poetic.

Must be the exhaustion causing the whimsical ramblings.

Had she come and gone already?

Disappointment, leaden and bitter, left a sour taste in his mouth.

He couldn't ask someone.

Too obvious.

Coburn was bloody right about him—he usually was, the irritating, confident arse.

Logan *was* an imbecile, caught neatly in his own trap.

This skulking around was unworthy of him and Mayra. Rash and stupid to not tell her his real identity. His ill-conceived impulse would make winning her more difficult. And each time they met and he continued the charade, it became harder to reveal the truth.

For God's sake, she was his betrothed.

He ought to ride straight to the Keep and claim her this instant. Except, his innocent boyhood vow yet echoed in his guilty conscience, and her repeated requests to have their betrothal ended intrigued as much as puzzled.

Mayra's last troublesome letter raised the stakes treacherously high.

Perfectly impersonal politesse, nonetheless, her missive held a distinct accusatory tone and suggested his constant neglect surely indicated a lack of interest in pursuing their union. And therefore, it would *behoove*—her word—them to end the *farce*—again, her word—with the greatest of alacrity.

Where did she come up with her expansive vocabulary?

Exceptionally well-read for a female, it seemed.

And then, by Odin's gnarly pointed teeth, she'd neatly—he imagined the clever smile twitching her lovely, kissable mouth—dropped the lode stone.

Square on Logan's unsuspecting head.

Mayra had written King George, too.

Saucy, brazen, unpredictable, vixen.

Could things get any pricklier?

Why was she so frantic? So determined?

Arranged marriages were common enough, and this union strengthened both clans.

Not that he was altogether keen on the concept of marrying a woman he didn't know. But since he'd been backed into a corner, he might as well look on the favorable aspects.

Truth to tell, since encountering her, his opinion toward the match had warmed several degrees.

And her beauty and wit haven't at all influenced

ye?

Not to mention the swell of satiny breasts he'd glimpsed above her bodice when he'd held her that first day. Aye, any *mon* still breathing—*dead too*—would count himself fortunate to take such a bonnie lass to wife.

Nevertheless, Logan couldn't quite reconcile the amiable woman he saved to the resolute lass who'd presumed to write the king. Some might even accuse her of imprudence or impertinence.

Shaking his head once, he skewed his mouth into a half-appreciative, half-cynical grin.

Suggesting to Logan he find a more suitable bride.

Damn, Mayra had a true Scotswoman's pluck and initiative. They were well-matched in that regard.

In other ways as well.

Namely, their mutual physical attraction, which multiplied each time he saw her.

His attention strayed outside—to the villagers rushing about, spearing fretful glances to the ominous sky—before he casually examined the men within the cozy taproom.

Had one of these men been Mayra's beau before he arrived in the village?

Something queer occurred behind his ribs, almost like the time he'd fallen from a branch as a child. He couldn't find his breath as an excruciating vice squeezed his chest. All he could do was wait for the terrifying sensation to pass.

Only this feeling wasn't altogether terrifying—just unfamiliar and gut-wrenchingly uncomfortable. It spread thick, dark, and choking, like smoke, filling his lungs, stealing his breath, and muddling his reasoning.

He sucked in a long, stabilizing breath.

His imagination was getting the better of him.

Surely the sensation couldn't be possessiveness or jealousy.

Most assuredly not.

He wasn't the jealous sort. At least… he hadn't been until now.

Until Mayra.

His eyelids half-lowered, Logan, nonetheless, examined each patron in turn.

Not a *mon* present that he deemed worthy of his

Mayra, and if any of these Scots were shy of their fortieth birthday, he'd gnaw his muddy, possibly manure-caked, boots.

According to MacPherson—the innkeeper had proved a ready wealth of information—Mayra was always well-chaperoned when she came to Glenliesh. And not only did she regularly give to the unfortunates, evidentially, her many attributes also included an acute intellect. She'd acted as Dunrangour's chief since her father's death, until her younger brother was old enough to succeed.

Oh, aye, his intended was quite an unexpectedly but delightfully complex woman.

Or ... artfully deceptive.

The unbidden sentiment wiggled its tenacious way into his contemplations.

Though MacPherson assured him Mayra was seldom out of her diligent chaperones' sights, Logan knew too well that loyal and devoted servants could be manipulated.

Particularly if they feared for their position.

What type of a mistress was Mayra?

As kind and sweet as his first impression indicated, or did she hide her true nature under false smiles and artificial demureness?

Rodena had.

Until she'd captured Da in her gossamer web, first sucking his integrity from him, bit by bit, and soon draining him of his joy, his pride, his money, and eventually, his will to live.

Livid didn't begin to describe his stepmum's reaction when he'd cut off her funds.

A satisfied grin pulled Logan's mouth upward as he wended his way between tables. No wonder she'd hied off to Edinburgh. However, he'd continue to provide for Isla, despite her questionable heritage. After all, the lass couldn't be faulted for her mum's infidelity, and she believed Da her father and Logan her brother.

Isla would never learn otherwise from him.

He wouldn't add cruelty to his growing list of sins.

Finding a secluded corner table, he sank into the scratched chair, and after extending his legs, raised a forefinger and signaled MacPherson.

"A pint and strong tea if ye have it."

"Aye, Mr. Wallace." MacPherson's jowls trembled as he trundled to the bar. "Right away."

Logan's attention drifted to the activity outside once more. An odd yellow-green tint edged the pregnant clouds. Orange lightening flashed an angry, jagged streak, moments before the heavens grumbled loudly.

Would Mayra come as promised?

God, he hoped so, for he longed to see her again. But the petulant sky didn't bode well, and she was almost certainly guaranteed a thorough soaking, and perhaps pelting from hail, too if she dared the journey.

Better for her to have stayed at the Keep in this weather.

In the days since they'd met, his mind had continually wound its way to pleasant musings about her. A few rather erotic daydreams too. That caused him no small amount of consternation.

In general, he didn't indulge in lewd imaginings about women.

For years, he'd ignored her, unforgivably, and he

shouldn't be a bit surprised that his inattention piqued her.

A great deal from the tenor of her letters. From the tone of her last note, ready to kick him head over arse or take a riding crop to him.

In his defense, he hadn't known of her many correspondences until he returned home.

Da confessed he'd been too distressed to forward them, afraid of Logan's reaction when he discovered Mayra was as opposed to the union as he. With the dowry gone, naught could be done now in any event.

Merely contemplating the ways her partial dowry might have benefited his clan caused unbidden ire to scuttle up his chest and close his throat.

With a weighty clunk, MacPherson set the tankard before Logan, foam dribbling over the pewter edge. A steaming cup of tea, a bowl of mutton stew, a plate with cold meats, cheese, sliced apples, and hard brown bread followed.

"Ye look like ye could use a bite. My Maggi makes the best stew, she does. And she said ye missed breakin' yer fast again t'day."

Distinct curiosity rang in the last few words, but MacPherson wouldn't ask why Logan left the inn before light each morn. Though it was outwardly a respectable establishment, he wouldn't be shocked to learn a nefarious transaction or two took place beneath the inn's gabled roof on any given day.

"Thanks. I appreciate it."

Logan wrapped a hand around the cup and promptly burned his fingertips. He blew on the tea before taking a tentative sip.

Hot and strong. Just how he liked his.

Taking another drink, he relished the warmth seeping to his middle. He hadn't realized how chilled he'd become and welcomed the tea's soothing heat chasing the nip away.

The door swung open, and a violent gust snatched the panel and slammed it against the wall.

Mrs. MacPherson uttered a startled squeak and wheeled toward the entrance, nearly dropping her full serving tray

Cheeks and nose glowing, and her hair a tousled mess, Mayra charged inside. After wrestling the door closed, she secured the latch and offered a weak, apologetic smile.

"I'm so sorry. The wind yanked the door right from my hands. I fear quite a storm is brewing. I'm not certain I'll be able to make it home."

"No' to worry, lass," Mrs. MacPherson assured her. "We've empty rooms. Lady Findlay would have my hide if I let ye even attempt such a thing. Did Reed see to old Horace for ye?"

"Aye," Mayra affirmed with a husky chuckle. "Horace actually trotted the last quarter mile, so eager was he to reach the village. I dinna remember the last time the auld laddie moved so fast."

Mrs. MacPherson bustled to a table and unloaded the foaming tankards to a trio of auld men hovering over a chessboard.

Vainly trying to secure the wayward spirally strands that had sprung loose from her coiffeure, Mayra inspected the room. Her perusal halted when her bright azure gaze landed on Logan. A merry smile lit her eyes and tipped her mouth as she swept to him while removing her gloves.

Without waiting to be invited, she pulled out the chair opposite him and gracefully sank onto the seat. Her plaid and skirts billowed around her, and after plopping her rather worn gloves atop the equally well-used table, she continued to try to restore order to her hair.

Giving a small, abashed shrug, she explained. "I tried a new hair style. As ye can see, it didna fare well in the wind. At least I was spared that."

She pointed to the sheets of rain falling in torrents and lashing the windows.

Already, water had turned the street to mud and formed miniature rivers along its length.

"I think ye look lovely, even with yer hair tumblin' down. I've never seen such a fair- haired Scot before."

Indulging the urge to touch the shimmering tangles, Logan dared flicked a silvery curl teasing her shoulder.

Not wise.

A few patrons and Mrs. MacPherson watched him and Mayra with keen interest.

Arms raised, Mayra paused in taming her hair.

Her mouth parted, and her surprised but definitely pleased gaze scooted to his. Darker blue rimmed her irises today, possible the effect of her pretty gown or her jovial mood.

"Ye, sir, are either a practiced liar, or a true gallant. For I caught a glimpse of myself in the window before I entered and this"—she pointed to her wild hair—"would cause the nag Cailleach to gnash her teeth in jealousy."

Mrs. MacPherson brushed the back of her hand across her brow. "Tea for ye, Miss Mayra? A Scotch pie too? I saved ye one."

"Och, Maggi. Ye're such a dear. Thank ye. I'm chilled through. And then would ye join us? If ye can spare a few minutes." Mayra gifted Mrs. MacPherson one of her brilliant smiles, and Logan's heart, or something in that vicinity, swelled with a joyful heat.

The minx had captivated him already.

How could that possibly be?

Mrs. MacPherson's curious gaze darted between Mayra and Logan.

No fool she.

"I'll fetch them for ye, and glad I'd be to rest my sore feet and enjoy a cuppa. Especially with a handsome young gentleman."

She winked and hurried away.

"I believe she's flirting with ye." Mayra chuckled, pushing one last pin into her hair. Winged brows peaked, she patted her head. "Do I look an absolute fright?"

"Nae such thing. Ye've managed to bring that bounty under control." Coburn levered his fingers toward her head. "Is that yer hair's natural curl?"

Her father's had been wavy, but nothing like the riot she'd just restrained.

"Aye, unfortunately," she agreed with a resigned nod. "And it gives me fits. Bettie too. Mum said I was bald as an egg until I was almost two, but when my hair did finally grow, it took on a life of its own."

He remembered the bald bairn.

She pulled a cute face. "I still remember them both trying to comb my tangles as a child. It took hours and hours. Or so it seemed."

He searched past her to the doorway. No cocky brothers or stern maid today. "Didna Bettie accompany ye?"

"Nae, the poor dear's still recovering, and my rascally brothers are confined to their chambers for hiding their tutor's clothing. Every last stitch, including his handkerchiefs and neckcloths."

Logan laughed and pulled his earlobe. He and Coburn had pulled a few antics like that with their unfortunate tutors too.

Unpinning the brooch holding her arisaid in place, Mayra cast him a saucy sidelong look, her mouth curving into a proud smile. "I came to Glenliesh on my own today."

The brooch's familiar blue stone glinted faintly as she laid the plaid over the chair beside her. She'd worn the Luckenbooth brooch each time he'd seen her. As a testament to everyone that she was affianced?

Assuredly not the behavior of a *bint* or an immoral lass.

Clutching the table's edge with long slender fingers, Mayra leaned forward, her sapphire eyes sparkling. My Laird, but she had the most expressive face and speaking eyes. A long tendril of hair she'd missed coiled across her nape.

"It's the first time. Ever. Can ye believe it? Me, nearly nineteen, and this is the only time I've been permitted the trip alone, even though Dunrangour is scarcely three miles away. I hope Mum will let me come by myself more often now."

He did too, for his time in the village must eventually come to an end, and he must win her over before it did. All of his other attempts to arrange an encounter with her had met with failure. She was well and truly supervised.

Mayra gave a slightly disgusted, or perhaps frustrated, shake of her head. "Do ye have any idea how annoying it is to be constantly chaperoned? It's bad enough that we so seldom get visitors. At times, I feel we live in a different country, for I have nae idea what happens elsewhere until months afterward."

Guarded so closely, no doubt she rarely spoke to a man alone, and yet the pleasure had been Logan's several times now. For whatever reason, for once, Fate seemed to have granted him favor.

He almost snorted aloud.

Was he actually giving Fate credit for any of this?

Fate whom he'd blamed and cursed soundly for decades about his lot in life?

Mayra's enthusiasm over such a simple thing, being permitted a solitary trip to the village, both pleased and concerned him.

Had her life truly been so stark as result of their mandated betrothal?

Why had her parents been so overly strict?

Teasing the fringes of Logan's hazy memory of the day he'd become betrothed to Mayra, a dim image emerged of Mrs. Findlay softly weeping into her daughter's bundled chest while Roderick Findlay's warrior-fierce glowers burned holes through Da and that other oily little man.

Logan remembered next to nothing of the king's agent except his great, awful stench and big yellow teeth. Like an over-sized mountain hare. Enough to give a child nightmares.

Aye, the Findlays hadn't been enthusiastic about

the arrangement, and who could blame them? They'd been forced to sacrifice their firstborn, and as it turned out, only daughter to a monarch's momentary fancy.

Da had never revealed why the king ordered the union. But given Mayra had been kept on a short tether. Attended constantly and allowed few of the social privileges a gently-bred woman was generally permitted, her parents must have been threatened with something calamitous to cause them to take such extremes.

A pang burgeoned, stabbing and burning in his chest.

He'd never considered Mayra's plight in the arrangement, only selfishly rebelled at his life having been manipulated by others.

Logan despised being a human pawn, and so too must she. And yet, wasn't he guilty as sin of doing the same thing this very moment by not being forthcoming?

Mayra touched her forefinger and thumb to the dainty pearl earbobs hanging from each delicate earlobe, checking the small gold clasps. "I do love coming to town, and I'm so looking forward to Edinburgh. We leave the day after tomorrow."

Tomorrow?

Damnation.

He wasn't ready to reveal the truth just yet.

Still, Logan had reason to be optimistic. His theory about a beau? Ground to powdery crumbs, and he couldn't be happier about it.

No woman so thrilled about a solitary sojourn to town carried on illicit assignations.

Ridiculously pleased at his conclusion, Logan lifted the tankard and halted his burgeoning smile by taking a swig.

"And when will ye return?" He'd use the time to look in on Lockelieth and explore that intriguing stretch of land supposedly hiding precious metals.

"Mum hasn't said for certain, but I imagine it will be toward the end of April."

That bloody long? He didn't have that much time to waste.

A contented sigh lifted Mayra's pert bosom, and giving a little wave, she smiled at an elderly man, half-asleep and smoking a pipe before the roaring stone fireplace. "He was our gardener until we couldn't afford—"

Catching her blunder, she stopped abruptly. Pink tinted her cheeks, and she fiddled with her gloves, straightening the fingertips.

So, the tattle of Dunrangour's financial woes was true.

That concerned Logan more than a little. Nevertheless, he changed the subject to avert her discomfort.

"That's an unusual clasp." He flicked a finger at the pin.

Would she tell him the truth of it? Why did her integrity matter when he was an unconscionable cur, lying to her?

Her attention followed his movements, and the joy drained from her face as her thick lashes fluttered closed for a fraction.

"It's... It was a gift to me when I was verra small. Mum insists I wear it."

Slowly she lifted her eyes, hesitation and

resolution reflected there and obvious in her partially-raised chin.

"Mr. Wallace—"

"Call me Coburn, please."

She sent a harried glance round the room and bent farther over, her bosom brushing the table's worn edge.

Lucky piece of furniture.

Cool hardness crept into her wisp of a voice and pleated the corners of her narrowed eyes.

"Coburn, I think ye should ken. As an infant, I was promised in marriage."

6

As the rain turned to hail, pelting the sodden earth with minuscule white cannon balls, Mayra held her breath and squeezed the table's rough edge until her knuckles turned white.

Every muscle taut, she awaited Coburn's response.

What would he say?

Would distaste or annoyance darken his mossy eyes and turn his handsome mouth down?

Would he care at all?

Had she presumed his attraction to her more than it actually was?

Or—*curses*—did his roguish, oh-so-charming demeanor hide a knave's heart and morals after all? In which case, she may have dived from a sizzling pan straight into the fire's flames.

Nae. Nae.

He was a good man.

An honorable man.

She could see it in his candid gaze. More than that, she sensed it.

Mayra had seriously considered lying, but in the end, Coburn must be made aware of her betrothal. Most everyone in the village knew, and if he hadn't heard already, he soon would.

He must also know she was determined to end the inconvenience.

Silly though it might be, she couldn't bear for him to think ill of her, to believe her dishonest or deceptive when Logan Rutherford's regard meant less to her than that little brown spider tending its web in the window's corner.

True, she scarcely knew Coburn, but something had transpired between them when he held her in his burly arms and had deepened with each mesmerizing encounter since.

Something wonderful. And frightening. And

unexplainable.

Yet, something that also made her want more from life and even more determined to escape the bondage she had lived with almost since birth. To dare to pursue a different path, understanding fully the consequences of her bold choice.

Was she brave enough to take that course?

Face the outcome, good or bad?

Pushing her shoulders back, she gave an inward nod.

Aye, mayhap not as much brave as desperate and resolute.

A puppet she'd be no more.

If the king didn't grant her request—if he even bothered to read her missive, since a Highland lass from an obscure clan was wholly insignificant to His Majesty—then Rutherford must be forced to cry off.

Almost seventeen, her eldest brother, Bhric, was the same age as Mayra had been when Da died and she took over as Dunrangour's temporary laird.

Past time Bhric assumed his birthright, and with Mayra's dowry, the growing Highland cattle herd, and the valuable land returned to Dunrangour's estate, Mum and the lads should be fine.

Coburn's large fingers, the nails clean and square, encircled his mug as he lifted it to his mouth. A shock of mahogany hair fell across his forehead, and he swept it back into place with his other hand, revealing a faded, whitish scar along the outside of his palm.

A childhood wound perchance?

She still knew little about him, except that he had the most musical Scots brogue and his eyes…. She became lost each time she looked into their depths.

Nevertheless, the unidentifiable feeling that took root in her soul days ago, continued to blossom and grow. So startling and rapidly, it quite took her breath away. Either she was smitten or deranged for entertaining the thoughts and desires he—an enthralling and striking stranger—had aroused.

He wore *Sassenach* clothing again today. She quite liked his dark tobacco-brown jacket. It emphasized his wide shoulders and brought out the brownish flecks in his eyes.

He'd never said what clan he called kin.

"Do ye ken him? The man ye're supposed to wed?"

After tearing off a piece of bread, Coburn popped it into his mouth.

"By that if ye mean, have I met him?" She gave a brief nod and shivered when the angry wind-born hail pummeled the window and a draft whisked over her, raising her flesh from neck to waist.

Or did premonition make her fine nape hairs tingle?

"Aye, I met him. Many years ago."

"But... I'm doing my utmost to have the agreement nullified. I winna willingly marry a man I only remember meeting but once in almost nineteen years. A man whose only interest, as far as I can discern, is my dowry and land. He won't even answer my letters."

Coburn swallowed and patted his mouth with his serviette, his manner hesitant. Or was that reservation?

"I'd like to call him a fool and condemn his thoughtlessness, but is it possible he didna receive them?"

At the intensity in his arresting eyes, she paused then frowned at the rumpled lace edging her bosom.

Could she possibly appear anymore disheveled and dowdy?

She straightened the scrap and inclined her head.

"I suppose so, but not likely. I've sent more than twenty over the course of three years. Da sent others. I have nae idea how many. And that still doesn't excuse the younger Rutherford ignoring me. Da said Rutherford agreed to court me or would ask to have the agreement voided. He's done neither."

A six year old lad agreed to those terms, her conscience admonished.

"Ignorin' ye is unconscionable, I'll admit. If he ken the beautiful, fascinatin', intriguin' woman sittin' opposite me this instant, trust me, he'd count himself a thousand times a fool."

Condemnation seeped into Coburn's voice as he fingered his knife handle.

Mayra almost missed the last part of what he said, having grown deliciously hot to her toes when he called her beautiful, fascinating, and intriguing.

Did he truly think so?

For he but echoed her thoughts about him.

Searching his handsome face, she examined each plane, every angle; the seductive dimple so quick to appear; his strong, chiseled jaw covered with that smattering of russet stubble she longed to brush her cheek against; his brow with its three narrow furrows; the crinkling at the corners of his eyes; and finally came to rest on his lips.

Coburn gently probed. "What will ye do, Mayra, if he refuses to release ye? He may have reason to do so ye ken no' of."

"I've written His Majesty as well, and I've decided upon a rather reckless course, if I'm forced to go that far. I ken verra little of my affianced, other than the lasses sigh over him, and I've heard he's rather a stickler for propriety." She crinkled her nose and brushed her fingers across her sleeve. "Any whisper of unseemliness or scandal, and he sniffs disdainfully, points his pompous nose in the air and marches away, stiff-arsed."

Coburn choked and slapped his serviette over his

face, coughing into it. Eyes watering, he managed to sputter, "Stiff-arsed?"

Mayra grinned and leaned low over the table once more.

"Ach, aye. Like a poker's been rammed up his— *Erm...* Well, ye take my meaning. Rutherford's verra pretentious. Plucks his brows, paints his face—pox scars, ye ken." She nodded knowingly. "He sniffs snuff. His wigs are said to harbor vermin—the tiny, creepy-crawly kind, and he wears gallons and gallons of scent, 'cause he doesn't bathe except twice a year."

She shuddered delicately and pinched her nose in mock horror.

Coburn's shout of laughter drew the other common room occupants' attention, and they smiled when he continued to laugh into his hand. Shoulders shaking, he shook his head and swiped the corners of his eyes.

"Good God. Nae wonder ye didna want to marry the sot. He sounds repulsive. If ye've never been outside Glenliesh, how do ye ken so much about him?"

Giving him an impish grin, she leaned back in her

chair and crossed her arms.

"I made all that up. Except the part about scandals. That much is true. The other is how I imagine him. Probably screams and jumps on a table when he sees a mouse or a toad, too."

"Undoubtedly. Likely swoons if he encounters an adder."

Coburn pushed his food aside, and leaned back in his chair, hooking an ankle over his knee.

She offered Maggi a bright smile as she bustled to their table, and whispered out the side of her mouth to Coburn, "I'd rather nae speak of him with Maggi here."

"Wise, I think."

Wouldn't do to have the curious servant be privy to their intimate conversation. And Maggi would never broach Mayra's betrothal, fully aware the subject distressed her.

Maggi set tea and a fresh Scotch pie, the pastry lightly browned, flaky, and scrumptious-smelling, in front of Mayra, then placed another cup before the empty chair beside her. The chair scraped as Maggi pulled it from the table, and once she'd plopped onto the seat and scooted it forward, she heaved a great sigh.

"I can only spare ye a few minutes. Since my Caronwyn married, I've been runnin' my tail feathers off, I have. She was a huge help with the cookin' and cleanin'. 'Specially the dishes."

Maggi jerked when thunder boomed loudly overhead, shaking the inn's rafters. "Foul as foul can be outdoors today."

Hail littered the mucky lane, and the afternoon sky, heavy with churning clouds occasionally lit with streaks of jagged lightening, sent long shadows into the inn. Two shingles blew off the blacksmith's roof a block down the street as the wind whistled and pounded against the common room's window panes.

Mayra took a sip of bracing tea, welcoming the warmth spreading from her stomach, soothing her frayed nerves. Her first time to town on her own and the worst spring storm in years descends.

Only an idiot would attempt to cross the street, let alone try to reach Dunrangour Tower in this.

All was not dismal, however.

Now, she had a legitimate excuse to linger with Coburn.

From the looks of the tempest, she might truly be forced to accept the MacPhersons' hospitality for the night. She hadn't funds with her to pay them, but she could send payment later. She'd not impose upon their generosity.

Pretending to adjust her serviette upon her lap, she observed Coburn chatting with Maggi.

He caught Mayra's subtle perusal and an enigmatic smile arced his lips.

Hours and hours of Coburn's pleasant company.

She couldn't imagine anything she'd prefer more.

"Please congratulate Carowyn for us. I have a small gift from Mum and me." Mayra bent and collected a brown paper wrapped package. "It's no' much, just embroidered handkerchiefs, and a crocheted doily."

"Ye and Lady Findlay needn't have done that, Miss Mayra." Maggi accepted the gift with a grateful smile.

Plunking four lumps of brown sugar into her cup, she gave Coburn the gimlet eye. As she stirred her tea, Maggi angled her head and continued to study him. "Mr. Wallace, ye remind me of someone. I cannae put my finger on who, but there's somethin' about yer eyes."

Coburn winked and dipped his spoon into his stew. "It's admiration for ye and yer fine cookin', Mrs. MacPherson." He tasted the soup and sighed dramatically. "Why, if ye weren't already married, I'd go down on one knee this verra moment."

Color blossomed on Maggi's cheeks, and she fluttered her work-reddened fingers at him. "Oh, pish posh. Ye're a born charmer, ye rogue."

"What's this? Wallace be ye flirtin' with my darlin' Mags?" Searc approached, wiping his hand on a towel. He gave his wife's shoulder a gentle squeeze. "My dear, I'm afeared the bread's burnin'."

"Och. I plum forgot. My mind's gone to puddin', it has." Maggi, as slender as her husband was round, sprang from her chair so quickly it would've toppled if he hadn't grabbed the back.

"Do either of ye need anythin' else?" MacPherson cast a worried eye to the nearly deserted street as the last of the patrons dared the hostile elements.

Only a young couple with a small child and two middling-aged gentleman—one who looked to be a cleric—remained. Likely overnight guests or travelers unwilling to brave the storm's wrath.

"I'm perfectly content for now, but thank ye." Mayra took a dainty bite of her pie. "As always, the best I've ever eaten. Someday, I'll have Maggi's recipe from her."

Had Coburn seen the innkeeper's pensive glance at his nearly empty establishment?

"I'm fine, as well."

"I want to make sure my lads have the stock and stable secure. This looks to be a fierce storm." MacPherson threw the towel over his beefy shoulder, frowning as a gust slammed into the inn, rattling the windows and sending the walls to trembling. "Miss Findlay, ye cannae return home in this. It's near dark as dusk already, and ye have the forest to travel through."

Despite the uncertainty marring her forehead, Mayra gave him a reassuring smile. "I ken. Maggi graciously said I might stay until the tempest passes. I'll have to send payment for the room later. I hope ye dinna mind. I dinna have more than a few shillings with me. I do hope Mum doesn't fret too much, but I ken she'd prefer I remain here where it's safe than try to reach home in this squall."

"Ye needn't worry about payment lass, and yer mum would want ye to stay." With a slight nod, MacPherson scuttled to the kitchen.

Lower lip clamped between her teeth and brows knitted, Mayra peered outside. "Do ye think I might try to make it home? Mum will fuss something awful if I dinna, and she mightn't let me ever come to town again on my own."

Assuredly she wouldn't. And besides, Mayra loathed spending money on a chamber when a perfectly comfortable bed awaited her at Dunrangour.

Lifting her head, her gaze landed on the two armchairs before the hearth.

She needn't accept a room from the MacPherson's

at all. She could wait out the storm before the fire.

Coburn laid his palm atop Mayra's, yanking her attention to him—to his big tan hand covering hers. "I think she'd want ye to be safe most of all. But if ye're really worried, I shall take ye."

The shrieking gale attacked the shutters, hammering them violently against the inn, and a wooden bucket hurtled down the street, bouncing end over end.

"Nae. Searc's right. Trees could crash down. I think it wisest to stay here."

Her gaze sank again to his hand still resting upon hers. Fine bronze hairs covered the knuckles and back.

"Coburn, I think I may have conceived a way to rid myself of Rutherford."

Did she dare tell him her reckless plan?

She barely knew him—*really knew him*—so why did she trust him so completely? Feel like she could share anything, and he'd understand?

Well, almost anything. Certainly not her blush-worthy musings regarding him.

Coburn spread her fingers, lacing his with hers,

and tipped his mouth upward, the seductive curve lighting his handsome face and turning her joints to jelly.

Mayra ought to pull away, but all thought of doing so vanished when he started rubbing his rough thumb slowly over the back of her hand. She couldn't tear her eyes from the simple yet intimate, hypnotic movement.

The rest of the room, the other occupants, faded into a distant haze, until it was just she and Coburn.

"I ken ye feel this between us, Mayra. It's too powerful to disregard. I think we've stumbled onto somethin' rare. So beautiful and precious, we mustn't ignore it."

Aye, impossible to ignore.

The desire and warmth in his rich, deep voice paled to the heat sparking in his hooded eyes.

Her nipples puckered in answer to the longing shimmering in his molten gaze.

Coburn raised her hand and brushed his lips across her knuckles in a swift, hot kiss, and an electric jolt raced up her arm.

Breathless, caught up in the moment, she didn't

care if anyone noticed.

"Aye, it defies understandin' because this gift came upon us so swiftly, but it's real. Tell me ye dinna feel it too, my bonnie, Mayra."

"Aye, but I dinna understand it," she shyly confessed. "We've only met these few times. I ken nothing about ye."

Still she didn't withdraw her hand. Instead, Mayra turned hers over so that their palms met, and her fingers—*the strumpets*—curled into his in the most natural clasp.

The knowledge he felt the same irresistible, irrational draw enveloped her in comfort and confidence.

And hope. Real, genuine, viable hope.

For the first time, she dared contemplate loving someone.

Coburn strayed his forefinger to her wrist, tracing a narrow, sensuous path.

She bit her lip when little sparks zipped along her nerves. How she wanted him to move higher, to trail his fingers up her arms, over the span of her neck...

Perhaps—heavens, her thoughts ran along a naughty path—brush the swell above her bodice.

"I have a solution too." He firmed his grasp on her hand, his eyes now a deep, mesmerizing forest green.

Did desire turn them that color?

Desire for her?

She wrenched her wayward attention back to what he'd said. "Solution?"

To what?

Och, aye, Logan Rutherford.

"Ye could marry me, Mayra. As soon as the storm passes, we could find a rector. In fact, I think that *mon* yonder," he jutted his head toward the quiet chap, "might be a cleric."

M ayra's breath stalled.

No wink or mocking smile accompanied Coburn's extraordinary statement.

What a scrumptious, novel solution, even if he did but jest.

Quite the most perfect, insane, absurd, and oh-so-tempting idea she'd heard in a great, great while.

Ever, truth be told.

But entirely impossible. Impractical. Unfeasible. *Dangerous.*

Even had he been serious, the risk was simply too vast.

To have Dunrangour, everything the Findlays owned, forfeited to the Crown and face imprisonment or worse?

No. Imprudent at best and catastrophic at worst.

She knew full well why Da and Mum had agreed to the union between her and Rutherford. They'd told her plainly, because they wanted her to know just how callous and treacherous her future father-in-law was, so she'd never trust the scunner.

She squeezed Coburn's broad, strong fingertips between hers. "I ken ye're teasing, Coburn. I'm sure ye've nae more desire than I to bring a monarch's wrath upon yer family or mine by defying a king's edict."

"Wrath? Surely nothin' so verra severe." His fingers continued to work their seductive magic.

For certain, wantonness flowed in her veins if she responded like this to the mere touch of his hand upon hers.

"Ye think no', Coburn?"

Her gaze riveted on their interlaced fingers, she debated whether to tell him all.

Why not?

And she could also discover whether he counted

the Rutherfords as friends. May a goose nip her bum if he did, for he'd not like what she had to say.

"Are ye acquainted with the Rutherfords of Lockelieth Keep?"

"Aye. I ken of them. Artair Rutherford died recently." Head canted, Coburn regarded her, his mien suddenly more reserved.

Mayra's jaw sagged, her spine going rigid.

"He did? His son, Logan, is my betrothed. How could we no' have heard?"

"It takes some families longer than others to talk about great loss, and ye've admitted, ye're rather secluded at Dunrangour." Coburn shrugged and resumed his sensual onslaught on her hand and wrist. "The news didna reach ye yet. That's all."

She well understood lingering grief. Mum yet mourned Da, and often her eyes still misted with sorrow. But Da had been a wonderful, loving father and husband, while Artair Rutherford...

Blast her stays, but a slow, heady fire tunneled through Mayra's veins. Deucedly difficult to concentrate on the important subject when her very bones were in danger of melting.

She swallowed and with some effort focused on the topic at hand. "Still, I would've thought Rutherford would have sent us word of something of such importance. Just another instance of his flagrant disregard, I suppose."

Would Logan be less inclined to grant her request or more, now that he was Lockelieth's laird? The emotional storm raging inside her exceeded the unrelenting tempest thrashing the Highlands.

"Mayra, what makes ye think breakin' the betrothal will raise King George's ire?"

At Coburn's soft question, she veered her attention from the tumultuous outdoors.

She sighed and peaked her brows high on her forehead for a resigned instant. "The king must approve the termination. Or if he winna, then Rutherford must be the one to cry off. I canna."

"Because...?" Coburn would have the whole torrid tale, it seemed.

Mayra finally withdrew her hand when Searc began lighting additional lamps and candles about the dim room. She'd been too bold already, and to continue to permit Coburn to fondle her hand atop the table was pure foolishness, no matter how splendid it might feel.

"It's nae a pretty tale, Coburn. At least no' the portion I've been told. But I have nae cause to doubt my parents."

The gentle upward melding of his lips spread tenderness across the carved planes of his dear face. Encouragement shone in his kind gaze. He was the type of man she could love, the type who tempted her to pelt responsibility and reason to next December.

And beyond.

"Tell me, Mayra. I want to ken everythin' about ye."

After an indecisive moment, she gave a small, reluctant nod. "I dinna wish to speak ill of the dead. But Artair Rutherford was a covetous cur, as well as an intimate confident of King William."

Coburn frowned, twin lines crinkling his forehead from temple to temple, and drawing his taut mouth into a stern line. "Why do ye believe that?"

"Rutherford whispered falsehoods in King William's ear about my Da's loyalty to the Crown. He went so far as to produce witnesses, attesting they'd heard Da's treasonous murmurings." A thread of bitterness seeped into her words. "All fabricated, paid-for lies, of course. But Da's great uncle *had* conspired decades before, and he swung from the gallows for his treachery."

All a rouser needed to stir fear was a strand of truth, no matter how farfetched and false the nefarious accusation.

Tense lines framing his mouth, Coburn rested his forearms on the table.

Maybe she shouldn't have revealed this ugliness. Perchance it was too soon. Or, perhaps, too off-putting.

"Please, go on," he prompted, just the merest bit of something—pain or regret?— deepening his voice.

"Mum said hatred and greed motivated Artair Rutherford to falsely accuse Da. To prove his loyalty to King William, my father was forced to agree to betroth me to Logan Rutherford. If he refused, Da faced imprisonment and confiscation of Dunrangour

Tower." Ire rang in her whispered words. "That would've left Mum and me destitute."

Unnaturally still, even guarded, Coburn regarded her keenly. Not accusing, exactly, but definitely assessing. "But why go to such efforts? Only a man with a vendetta or one unhinged takes those measures, and I dinna believe Rutherford was off his heid."

Mayra smoothed an eyebrow, then touched two fingers to her chin, searching her memory for the details.

"At one time, Artair Rutherford had been betrothed to Da's sister, and the same valuable property dowered to me had also been a part of Aunt Astrid's settlement. I dinna believe it was mere chance my settlement included the same acres. Artair verra specifically demanded that provision both times."

Listening intently, Coburn's eyes narrowed until only the irises showed. "Is the property especially valuable?"

Mayra hitched one shoulder and rubbed her hands over her arms when another gust seeped through the inn's siding. "I dinna really ken. Supposedly, years ago, someone found evidence of copper and silver ore. Da always said he planned to explore the possibility of mining the crags before he was forced to settle the land on me. He couldn't touch it afterward."

"Why didna Artair and Astrid marry?" Coburn tapped his long fingers atop the table, his expression bland.

So, why did she have the impression he fumed inwardly?

Mayhap she'd made a huge mistake in telling him everything.

Well, if this put him off, then he wasn't the *mon* she'd believed. He might as well know the rest, and then she'd know if she'd misjudged him after all.

She'd hoped—*believed*—he might not care about the unsavory rumors and whispers shadowing the Findlays for generations.

Such disenchantment engulfed Mayra, she feared she might be ill, and she took a hasty gulp of tepid tea to wash the bitterness from her mouth.

"A mere month before their wedding, Astrid eloped with a gypsy traveler," Mayra said. "The notes she sent Artair and our family said she loved the traveler and carried his bairn. She died giving birth, and the wee bairn died too."

Mayra had learned the sordid tale when Da lay dying.

He'd begged her to forgive him for promising her to Logan Rutherford.

Of course, she'd forgiven him. He'd only tried to protect her and Mum. And later, his sons.

"So ye believe revenge motivated the elder Rutherford to falsely accuse yer father and force him to agree to troth ye to Logan?" Something like pained disbelief frayed the edges of Coburn's lowered voice.

She slanted her head and shied her brows upward in affirmation.

"Aye. I do. Revenge and greed. Artair Rutherford maintained Aunt Astrid's settlement was his since their betrothal was never terminated before she died. There was nae legal basis for his claim, and according to my parents, he was infuriated when denied the property."

"It seems there's a great deal about Artair Rutherford I never kent." Jaw taut, Coburn skimmed his fingers over his strong chin and veered his troubled gaze outside, now enclosed in night's garments as nature continued to wreak her havoc.

Several lengthy, silent moments passed, as he remained absorbed in whatever thoughts consumed him. Mayra wrestled with her decision to share all.

Had it been a disastrous mistake?

Suppressing the despondency rising high from her belly, and emboldened by her decision to pioneer her own destiny, she cleared her throat. Her voice a mere husky shred, she murmured, "I confess, I'm grateful for yonder wicked weather if it means I might enjoy yer company longer."

Coburn's mouth swept upward, tenderness softening his handsome features.

"And I yers. Please, join me before the fire, and tell me of this plan of yers to escape Rutherford."

Logan withdrew his watch and examined the face in

the dancing firelight.

Nearly half past one.

The MacPhersons and the other guests had long since retired, and even the storm waned as if spent from the hours of assaulting the earth in its furious tantrum.

Delicate moonbeams stretched outward from the crisp moon, all the more brilliant in the storm-scrubbed sky.

He yawned behind one hand, flicking the timepiece cover shut with the other.

Melancholy, blacker than the Earl of Hell's waistcoat, pulled his mouth downward. His father had been a covetous, manipulating blackguard. Honor, it seemed, was a rare commodity, and Logan's own behavior wasn't above reproach either.

As much as he wanted to believe everything Mayra had told him was a vast, fabricated lie, in his gut, in the depths of his soul, he knew she spoke the truth. It explained so much, yet he couldn't bring himself to hate or revile Da.

Logan grazed a hand across his bristly face and

released a long, irregular breath.

"What am I to do about ye, Mayra Findlay?"

If only there were a way to make things right.

The how of it escaped him, nevertheless.

He couldn't see an alternative to the path he and Mayra had been set upon so many years ago.

Logan ran his thumbnail across the watch's silver case embossed with the family crest. The reverse side boasted the Rutherford motto: *Nec sorte, ne facto*— Neither by chance nor destiny.

His focus strayed to Mayra again, asleep on the other chair, her feet tucked beneath her and one slim hand cradling her cheek. Her full, creamy breasts surged upward, threatening to spill from her gown's bodice.

Neither by chance nor destiny.

Choice then?

Their betrothal at an age neither was old enough to understand or object to.

Their encounter that first day she'd tumbled from the cart.

Today's storm, forcing Mayra to stay in town.

Their obvious, immediate attraction to each other.

Far more by chance or destiny rather than a deliberate choice explained each of those circumstances.

And absolutely countered all that was rational.

Sitting there, watching the slow rise and fall of her chest, her slightly parted mouth, and the occasional flicker of her lashes fanning her cheeks, a peace unlike anything he'd experienced encompassed him.

The law proclaimed her already his, and now more than ever, he was determined she would be.

Her little cockeyed, elfin smile, the playful way she tilted her head when she listened, the way her eyes glowed with enthusiasm when she had something she wanted to say. Each characteristic, delightful and endearing, and each wrapped him more snugly, more securely, and inescapably in the web he'd spun.

Her plan was simple and straightforward.

Create a scandal and force him to put her aside.

Except after spending the day with her, growing more enchanted by the moment with the beautiful, witty lass, that was the last thing he meant to do. More determined now than ever to make her Lady Rutherford, he weighed his options.

He had but one.

He must tell her the truth.

Tomorrow.

Logan stood, and after banking the fire, gathered their belongings. He secured everything within her arisaid, and tied the corners together into a makeshift pack. He'd retained a room for her when she went to use the necessary. It was across from his at the third floor passage's far end, where he could make sure she was safe.

Though few guests lodged at the inn tonight, he'd not take a chance.

After sliding the crook of his elbow into the loop he'd created in the plaid, he scooped Mayra into his arms.

Although she opened her eyes for an instant, giving him a sleepy—*damn my eyes*—almost a seductive smile, after looping her slender arms around his neck, she shut her lids and resumed her contented slumber.

As he carried her up the flights, welcoming her weight and the chance to hold her close, every now and again she murmured in her sleep. Winded by the time he trudged up the last riser, he adjusted her and managed to push the latch to her door without dumping her onto the floor.

Though only just, as she tilted dangerously, and her head came within an inch of smacking the doorframe.

Casanova, he was not, and neither had he experience toting lovely women to bedchambers. He kicked the door closed and Mayra clung tighter, evidently believing the trek upstairs part of her dream.

"I've never been kissed," she sighed against his neck, her words sleep-thickened and garbled.

Her silky lips rasped against his flesh, and he flexed his jaw against the current of electric desire pounding along his veins.

He dropped Mayra's plaid on the chamber's single chair situated below the window, and in the moon's muddled half-light managed to bump his way to the bed. He tried to lay her down, but she clung to him, and in the throes of her dream, kissed his neck, then his jaw. And finally, her lips found his.

So incredibly sweet.

God help him, he shouldn't.

His pathetic honor, what remnant remained, screeched in offense.

Logan sank onto the bed, still snuggling her, and succumbed to temptation, feathering tiny kisses across her smooth brow, her silky lashes, the oh-so-sensitive tendon behind her ear.

"Coburn, kiss me. Really kiss me."

She moaned, that throaty, feminine, purr-like rumble which sent lust pounding to every pore.

He untwined her arms, and his chest heaving from self-restraint, Logan shook his head, though even if she'd been awake, she couldn't have seen much more than the shadowy movement.

"Lass, God kens I'm no' perfect, but I dinna ravish sleepin' maids."

"I'm no' asleep."

She giggled and turned onto her side. "I awoke when ye practically dumped me onto the floor."

Slanting a glance to the window, she hid a delicate yawn behind her hand. "The storm has come to an end?"

The tempest outside.

The one raging within him showed no sign of abating. "Aye, and the moon has come out in all her glittering finery to celebrate."

He lit the single taper atop the humble nightstand, needing a moment to perform the mundane task to bring his stampeding ardor under control.

Reaching up, she traced a trembling finger along his jaw.

"I do want to kiss ye, Coburn. Verra much, in fact. Is that wrong? Does that make me wicked?" She stilled her timid exploration, and curled her finger into her fist before slowing withdrawing her hand and dropping her gaze to the flickering candle.

"I suppose it does, doesn't it? I'm promised to another."

Tell her the truth.

Logan caught her hand and brought it to his mouth. He brushed his lips across the knuckles. "Nae, it dinna make ye wicked, lass. It makes ye young and healthy with a woman's desires."

Her luminous gaze gravitated to his. No guile or coyness shone in her beautiful blue eyes as she slanted her head in her quaint pixy way, her eyes probing to the depths of his soul.

"And do ye desire me, Coburn?"

Did he draw air to breathe?

Did he need food and water to live?

Did the moon, even now, light the heavens with silvery brilliance, almost equal to Mayra's tumbled tresses, spilling over her shoulders and back, cascading down her arms?

"Aye, lass. I desire ye." And his heart? What was happening to that organ? Something he'd never anticipated. "The scorchin' blood in my veins sings with want for ye."

Even as he spoke, he stretched out beside her and gathered her in his embrace. Inhaling her intoxicating floral scent, he nuzzled her neck and brushed his hands over her curvaceous hips and gently sloping thighs.

Foolishness. Insanity.

Absolute, glorious stupidity.

Mayra cupped his face with her soft palm and touched her lips to his chin. "Is that what I feel for ye? This strange, unnamed yearning? Is that why, even though we scarcely ken each other, I cannot rid my thoughts of ye, and why my stomach and heart flutter in the most peculiar manner when I'm with ye?"

How had she vocalized exactly what he experienced too, as inconceivable as that might be?

Some might call it lust, and surely carnal desire bubbled within. But he'd known physical hunger before, and this was something impossibly more.

He kissed her forehead, such tenderness throttling up his throat, he swallowed against the emotion.

"I think, perhaps, we've had somethin' rare and unexplainable occur, lass."

Tell her!

Mayra arched her neck, giving him access to the pearly column. "And what is that?"

Her question ended on a husky sigh when he glided his fingertips across her puckered nipple.

"I would make ye mine for all time Mayra, lass.

I've fallen in love with ye. My verra soul craves yer presence. Ye make me feel whole."

The full brilliance of her smile blossomed across her face.

"Aye, and I ye, Coburn. I dinna understand how 'tis possible in so short a time, but I winna deny it." Her joy faded almost as quickly, and her pretty mouth turned down. "But, I cannae be with ye, in that way. No' when I legally belong to another."

He took a steadying breath, prepared to tell all.

"Mayra—"

Her pleading look and the fingertips she touched to his lips muzzled him.

"I want to, believe me, I do with all my heart. It just that my entire life it's been drilled into me that I'm Rutherford's, and though I owe him nothing—loathe the man, truth to tell—I cannae betray him in that way." Her husky voice caught on a dry sob, and turning her head away, she pressed the fingertips of the other hand to her lips.

Happiness, bittersweet and pungent, wrapped around him.

God, how he loved her for her faithfulness. Yet part of him wanted her to hurl common sense and restraint aside and give herself to him despite the rashness or certain repercussions.

He kissed the fingers touching his mouth before gathering her near.

"Ah, my love. My precious love. All will be well. Somehow, I vow, I shall make it so," Logan said. "Now sleep. I'll watch over ye and leave before first light so nae tongues wag."

Then for God's sake, mon, tell her the damned truth!

Logan couldn't.

Not yet.

Not now.

Mayra loathed Rutherford.

No.

She loathed *him*.

8

Twice during the night Mayra awoke, each time nestled securely in Coburn's solid, wonderfully-scented embrace, his shoulder pillowing her head. She smiled and cuddled closer, hardly daring to believe this marvelous specimen of manhood loved her.

Seems 'twas her fate to love a highland rogue after all.

What a magnificent destiny.

Chin resting on her cupped hand, she gloried in the luxury of examining him as he slept.

Hair mussed, his dark lashes fanning his high cheeks, he appeared younger, contented. Yet, what did she know of this stranger who'd so easily captured her heart?

In all their conversations, he'd never even revealed what brought him to Glenliesh.

Wisdom demanded she at least discover something more than he was an only child and had no kin, save a dear cousin, and that he'd traveled these three years past. But then again, wisdom for all its benefits, didn't have a heart or soul. And therefore, wisdom couldn't possibly conceive how a person knew when they'd found their mate.

The third time she wakened, the sun shone bright in the morning sky, and Coburn's side of the bed was empty.

Heavens!

She bolted upright and shook her hair off her shoulders.

What time was it?

Through the window, she studied the sun's placement and scrutinized the cloudless heavens once more.

Mayhap eight?

The hour wasn't so very advanced then, but later than her typical six o'clock rising time.

That was what came of staying up and talking until the wee morning hours. She climbed from the bed, and stretching her arms overhead, smiled with pure joy. Her mouth remained tipped upward as she futilely attempted to smooth her wrinkled gown.

Coburn had left as promised, more concerned with her reputation than she.

If he'd been discovered in the chamber with her, surely Rutherford would've called off the wedding. Her reputation would've been shredded, of course. But what did that matter when Coburn wanted to marry her?

Except—

He hadn't actually said that he wanted to wed her. Only that he loved her and wanted to make her his.

Had she made a colossal mistake in judgement last night, sharing a bed, no matter how innocent?

What if...

She could scarcely form the thought.

What if he were married already?

God, why hadn't that occurred to her before?

Nae. Nae!

She wouldn't believe it of him.

Coburn could've taken advantage of her.

She'd wanted him to, and yet after she'd explained why she couldn't be intimate with him, he'd acted the gentleman. Well, fine, perhaps not a perfect gentleman, because he could've as easily slept outside her door, but he hadn't imposed himself on her.

More's the pity.

She chuckled and, arms extended spun in a gleeful circle.

What a wanton she'd become.

After washing her face and rinsing her teeth, she ran her fingers through her wild tresses.

No use.

She normally plaited her hair before sleeping. The best she could hope for was to constrain the mass. As she tried to find her scattered hair pins, then bring the springy curls that called themselves her hair under control, she worried her lower lip.

What about the dowry?

Was it forfeit if she was disgraced?

Ballocks and bluebells.

Why hadn't she considered that before too?

She'd never read the dafty settlement. Everything—*everything*—hinged on the dowered portions being returned to Dunrangour.

As soon as she returned home, she needed to see the contract.

Worrying her lower lip, she strolled to the window and scanned the horizon.

She should be on her way.

Mum and Bettie, and the boys too, would've worked themselves into a proper worry by now. In fact, Mum had likely dispatched clansmen to the village already. Surprising she hadn't sent them last night, truth be told.

Except, she'd known Mayra always visited Maggi MacPherson, and sometimes, more often than she ought since Da died, Mum indulged in laudanum a bit too freely. She mightn't have realized Mayra hadn't returned home until this morning.

If only Mayra dared defy the edict and marry another like Aunt Astrid had.

By all the wriggling eels in Loch Tolhorf, that

would solve the dowry problem. But then, what became of Dunrangour? Mum and the boys?

Would King George punish them and Coburn, too?

From his pompous English throne, would His Majesty care in the least about two Highland clans' issues?

She heaved a frustrated sigh. The risk to them was simply too great to take.

A soft knock interrupted her unsettled musings.

"Aye? Come in."

Coburn, his hair damp, his green eyes snapping with happiness stepped part way inside. "I have breakfast awaitin' us below. Then I'll accompany ye home. I must speak with yer mum."

"Why?" Mayra paused in collecting her arisaid, hanging over the chair's back.

Coburn cocked his head boyishly, a teasing grin crimping his mouth.

"Why do I have breakfast below?"

"Nae, why do ye want to speak with my mum, ye daft *mon*?" Laughing, she threw a pillow at him, and he ducked.

"Because I intend to ask her for yer hand in marriage."

Jaw unhinged and mouth gone dry, Mayra went still as stone.

Oh, if only it could be so.

"It's no' possible without the king's consent, Coburn."

"It *is* possible. Will ye trust me *leannan*?"

Sweetheart.

She swallowed and gave a short, uncertain nod.

As he touched her cheek and traced a path to her lips, his penetrating gaze sent a message she couldn't understand before he drew her into his arms whispering in her unruly hair. "There's somethin' I should've told ye when we first met. Somethin' I've tried to tell ye many times."

She shut her eyes, swathed in contentment and savoring the precious moment until rapid hoof beats, stampeding into the village, drew her attention to the small window.

Aye, indeed. Mum was in a right royal fuss and

froth.

Six Dunrangour clansmen trotted their mounts straight to The Dozing Stag.

"My clansmen are here. I'd expected as much."

If she stayed in this chamber with Coburn, she'd have her scandal.

Indecision plucked her nerves like taut harp strings before she filled her lungs with a revitalizing breath.

Mayra whirled away from him and the window.

She couldn't so easily bring disgrace on the Findlay name and her clan after all.

So she'd give Coburn his chance with Mum, and then if that failed, only then would she resort to ruination.

Draping her arisaid about her shoulders, she hurried to the door. "Ye can call this afternoon. I'll try to prepare Mum, though be warned, she'll no' easily be swayed. She's lived in fear for so long, I dinna think she'll be amendable."

"Mayra, wait." His face taut, Coburn held out his hand, palm upward. "There's somethin' important I really must tell ye."

The echo of booted feet hammering up the stairs filtered into the chamber.

"Miss Mayra?" called a familiar voice.

Fergus, Dunrangour's war chief, and Da's closest friend.

She sent Coburn a panicked glance.

"It's all right." He came to her and after clasping her hand, offered a reassuring smile. "We'll face them together."

Och, nae help for it now.

Scandal was upon her.

Mayra backed away from the door a few paces. "I'm in here, Fergus."

Coburn squared his shoulders and notched his chin upward like a general about to enter the battlefield.

Fergus and Hamish strode into the chamber, stopping short upon spying Coburn. Fergus's wary gaze sank to Mayra's fingers entwined with Coburn's.

"By Odin's bones, ye're the last person I expected to see," Fergus said, his eyes wide with astonishment and disbelief.

Eyes faintly squinted, Mayra swung her gaze from man to man. "Ye ken each other?"

Not impossible. She just hadn't anticipated it. More fool she.

"Aye." Hamish tilted his head a fraction, appearing none too pleased at the admittance. "I'd have recognized ye anywhere, Rutherford. Even if it has been nigh on to three-and-a-half years since I was banished by yer sire from settin' foot on Lockelieth's land again."

Oh, for goodness sake. They'd confused him for Logan.

To alleviate Fergus's and Hamish's scowls, Mayra withdrew her hand from Coburn's.

"Ye're mistaken, Hamish," Mayra said. "He's Coburn Wallace, no' Rutherford."

She finished securing the Luckenbooth brooch at her breast for the last time. After this morning, she'd never wear it again. It would be returned to Rutherford.

Fergus's grizzly eyebrows made a slow ascent up his broad forehead, and he cast Coburn an accusatory glare. "Nae, lass, he isna. He's Logan Rutherford. I'd swear my life on it. Coburn Wallace be his cousin."

A lethargic fog engulfed Mayra, slowing her heartbeat, muffling her hearing, distorting her vision. In trance-like disbelief, she blinked and shook her head.

Surely she'd heard wrong.

Fergus hadn't vowed Coburn was Rutherford? Had he?

As in Logan Rutherford.

Her betrothed.

Oh, God, nae. Please dinna let it be so.

She jerked her head to look at Coburn, seeing the answer in his grim countenance and speaking eyes.

He'd been impersonating his cousin.

She closed her eyes against the entreaty in his.

Charlatan! Liar!

"Please, Mayra. Let me explain."

He reached for her hand again, but she tucked her arms tight to her chest and retreated a pair of steps.

"Aye, somebody better be about explainin'," Hamish grumbled, his arms akimbo as he exchanged a severe glance with Fergus. "Yer mum's frantic, and she didna mention anythin' about yer meetin' yer betrothed in the village."

His eyes, usually a toasty brown, narrowed a wee bit, just this side of condemnation.

"That's 'cause she didna ken, did she, lass?" Fergus's gentle question hung suspended.

No, Mum didn't know. But neither had Mayra.

Nonetheless, she realized how guilty she and Co— Logan appeared, and if she'd been able to draw a decent breath, she'd have laughed at the irony.

Clandestine meetings with her affianced.

The stuff of sordid tales.

And what's more, she'd stupidly fallen in love with him. A man she'd convinced herself was a worthless sot.

He's nae a worthless sot.

He's a lyin' scunner.

Deceiver. Cull. Scoundrel. Rogue.

And, to her absolute consternation, even amidst his gut-wrenching treachery, he was still the man she loved with every excruciating breath she drew. One's heart didn't stop loving someone simply because their name changed.

However, it could, in the span of a heartbeat, stop trusting and believing.

After commanding her thoughts and stomach to cease their pitching, she inhaled a great gulp of fortifying air. Gradually releasing it, she angled her head.

"Hamish, Fergus, would ye please give me a moment alone with..."

Mayra couldn't call him Logan.

In her mind he was still Coburn.

From the corner of her eye, she saw the frown framing his firm mouth and the lines creasing his forehead over the slightly hooded gaze regarding her.

"Please give us a moment alone," she managed, righteous anger giving her strength.

Flinty faces unyielding, neither of her clansmen seemed inclined to move a muscle of their hulking, imposing forms.

Another time, she might have appreciated their protectiveness. But not when the tight rein she held on her composure, threatened to plummet over the humiliating precipice of hysterics.

"Ye may wait in the passageway, outside the door. I'll only be a few moments."

Mayra would have her say with... Logan.

How could she ever become accustomed to that name for him?

She'd harbored resentment for so long, and it had colored Logan Rutherford as a heartless, selfish knave. Her mind couldn't reconcile that personality with the marvelous *mon* before her that she'd come to know and love.

"I give my word as a Scot, she has nothin' to fear from me." Logan unflinchingly met her champions' stony gazes.

Nothing in their steely countenances yielded a jot.

"Five minutes, is all I require," he said, his expression every bit as unyielding.

To do what?

"I am still her betrothed," Logan reminded them, a trifle more force behind his words.

God rot his handsome face, he was.

Their reluctance as obvious as their disapproval,

Fergus and Hamish shuffled from the room, and shut the door behind their broad backs.

Mayra hadn't a doubt they stood directly outside the door, probably had their ears pressed to the course slats, truth be told.

Both looked ready to pound Rutherford to next March.

She'd like to clout him in his aristocratic nose, too.

Mayra wandered to the window, and after presenting her back, pressed her fingers between her eyes for a moment.

She wouldn't cry.

Nonetheless, such a painful ache burgeoned from her belly, traveling up her constricted chest and tight throat, she could hardly summon one anguished, whispered word.

"Why?"

"Mayra, my precious bonnie lass." Emotion deepened the timbre of his voice.

Logan crossed to stand behind her, a tempting wall of virile masculinity.

The heat of his body enshrouded her as did his scent.

Then he settled his big, yet wonderfully gentle hands on her shoulders, and rather than railing her indignation, she yearned to turn into his embrace and weep like a bairn.

Instead, she stiffened her spine and shoulders and shrugged off his hands. Out of self-preservation, she kept her back to him. For if she looked into his eyes, those mesmerizing hazel pools, she feared she'd weaken and succumb to her feckless heart.

And right now, this instant, her mind and her indignation insisted on answers.

"Why?"

She sent the briefest of glances over her shoulder before gripping the window sill, her knuckles white from the pressure.

"I need to understand why ye deceived me, Logan, when the truth would have served us both so much better."

"Because I'm an idiot. I kent ye desperately wanted out of the betrothal, and I couldn't honor yer request." Logan's long sigh warmed her nape, he stood so close.

Couldn't or wouldn't?

A vast difference between the two. "Why no'?"

"My da spent the dowry entrusted to his care. I don't have the monies to replace it. It fact, Lockelieth totters on financial ruin. To save her, we must wed verra soon, so I can claim the rest of the dowry."

Nae.

Mouth parted in shock and dismay, Mayra whipped around.

"He spent it? *All* of it?" she whispered, through the tightness choking her throat. "And Lockelieth still faces ruin. How can that be?"

Scorching, stubborn tears welled, but just as obstinately, she blinked them away.

She understood full well what this meant. Damn Artair Rutherford's corrupt soul.

Outraged fury wrestled with reason until common sense, heavily tinged with bitterness, prevailed.

"Ye could've simply told me as much, Logan. Been honest with me. At least after the first time we met. But to carry on the charade..." Mayra shook her head, and several curls toppled loose.

Stupid, diddy hair. She'd cut it off above her ears!

He caught one tendril between his fingers and tugging it ever so gently, pulled her into his arms.

Outside the door, the floorboards squeaked, and a wry smile quirked one side of her mouth.

Fergus and Hamish were certainly getting an earful.

"Ye're right. And in hindsight, my excuse seems feeble. Even to me. I ken that now. I meant to tell ye. I was stupid and weak and a fool." His nostrils flared before he pressed a tender kiss to her forehead. "But... I was afraid."

Her brawny, powerful highland rogue afraid?

"Of what? That, I couldn't love the real ye? Ye never gave me a chance to do so. What we have," Mayra waffled her hand between them, "has been built on a lie. I dinna ken what's real anymore."

She felt violated and exposed. But worst of all, she'd been made to admit to herself, she couldn't trust her instincts.

What was she to do now?

Her greatest hope of returning Dunrangour to prosperity had been blasted to smithereens, as had any hope of nullifying their betrothal.

And even that notion had her thoughts tumbling about in confusion.

Vulnerability she'd never seen before shadowed Logan's face. He shifted his attention over her head to gaze outside, and his throat worked for a moment before he spoke again.

"Aye, I dreaded ye'd loathe me, Mayra. But more than that, I feared yer loyalty, feared to trust ye. Then I fell in love with ye, and above all else, that terrified me to my marrow. Love bewitches and befuddles, makes even the most decent, logical of men do stupid, rash, asinine things."

Two heavy raps rattled the door, demanding her attention, and she tossed a frustrated glance over shoulder.

"It's been more than five minutes," Fergus said, his tone just short of a growl.

"Just a few more moments." She cocked her head

at Logan's cynicism. "Ye make love sound like a putrid disease to be avoided."

Logan veered her a swift, sidelong glance before returning his perusal to the street filling with villagers going about their daily routines.

"My father's wife betrayed him with countless men. Rodena bore a wee lass, Isla, that wasn't a product of my father's loins. I was determined no' to allow my emotions to rule my head and turn me into a lovesick dobber as he had. He lost sight of all that he valued. His integrity, his honor, his self-respect. She destroyed him. It was Rodena who convinced Da to squander yer dowry."

Even with her heart fragmented, her soul battered from his duplicity, Mayra understood Logan's reluctance, although she couldn't agree with his reasoning.

"I dinna believe love does that to everyone. Perhaps those with weak, spineless characters." Which Artair Rutherford had proven he possessed. "But love also has the ability to strengthen. To fortify. To encourage greatness. My parents' marriage was a perfect example of that."

"Aye. Ye're right. It's difficult and painful to admit my father wasn't the man I thought he was." He met her gaze, his resolute. "But I vow to ye, I am no' him."

"And I'm no' yer stepmum." Hadn't she demonstrated her virtuousness already?

A wry half-smile quirked Logan's mouth upward on one side. "Can I ask why ye've been so determined to end our betrothal? Is it because ye didna want to marry a stranger, or is there somethin' more?"

Mayra hunched a shoulder an inch, sadness and marrow-deep disappointment a heavy mantle upon her.

"It was partially because I didna want to marry a man I didna ken. One I mistakenly believed a callous cull." She cut him a contrite glance.

"Mayra—"

She raised her palm to him. "Please. Let me finish."

"Aye. Go on then," Logan said.

"I've never been a silly female who dreamed of a knight or a prince carrying her off on a white horse to live blissfully ever after." She tucked a curl behind her ear, her attention beyond the window. "But since Da died, it's been because I couldn't fathom another way to save Dunrangour except to use the dowry. However, unlike the portion trusted to yer father's care, the other half has remained intact."

Logan touched her shoulder for a brief moment. "I believe I have a solution for that, which would also help the villagers and restore Lockelieth. I want to start a minin' venture on the land that's part of yer settlement."

"That's a lofty goal." And though noble, it did little to appease her profound disenchantment.

Excitement lit his countenance, and eagerness inflected his voice. "I believe the adjacent acres are also silver and copper rich. I've had a letter from my cousin who says there are also tin and coal deposits in the region. We'd need the rest of yer dowry to start the undertaking, but I've also several investments that I hope will begin producin' a solid income within a year."

"Ye've thought this out, it seems."

If what Logan said were true, then at least she didn't have to fear for Dunrangour's or her family's future.

Just her own, which looked precarious at best.

Logan brought her hands to his mouth and pressed his lips for a long moment to first the knuckles of one hand, then the other.

"Can ye forgive me, Mayra? Give our love a chance? Let me make amends? Prove that ye can trust me?"

"Forgive ye? Aye. In time, I have nae doubt I can. I dinna hold grudges. However, trust ye? Nae. That I canna vow. Trust canna be rekindled as simply as putting a spark to tinder." She snapped her fingers before his face, permitting her hurt to speak.

He bowed his neck. "Ye're right, of course."

"And, I believe a marriage without trust, even an arranged one, is worse than a union without love. I've been forthright with ye from the verra beginning, Logan. I told ye I was betrothed. I told ye I'd considered creating a scandal, and," she lowered her voice so Fergus and Hamish couldn't hear her confession, "I didna give myself to ye, because my honor wouldn't permit it."

"And I love ye all the more for each of those. I ken I dinna deserve ye. Nevertheless, please, believe me when I say that above all else, I would make ye my wife. No' because a paper says we must, but because I canna imagine my life without ye now."

Entreaty and sincerity sharpened the contours of Logan's dear face, but the moisture filling the corners of his eyes nearly undid Mayra.

Yet, for weeks he'd lied, and that she couldn't easily forget or put aside. She respected herself too much.

Righteous anger prompted her words, even as the door shuddered when either Hamish or Fergus bumped it.

"For all of yer pretty professions, unless His Majesty releases us, ye ken as well as I that I've nae choice but to wed ye." Mayra was right back where she started, mere weeks ago, only now her heart was no longer her own.

An auburn-haired rogue, whether he deserved it or

not, had laid claim to the bruised organ.

One hand on his nape, Logan tucked his head to his chest, remaining silent for a long moment before raising his gaze to snare hers. "Aye, what ye say is true. Tell me what ye would have me do then, sweet lass? Naught but yer happiness matters to me. I shall write King George, too, if that is what ye wish, though we both ken he mightn't even respond."

The door trembled again.

For certain, the great gollumpuses waiting in the corridor could use a dose of patience.

Mayra stepped away from Logan, and after gathering her gloves and hat, faced him.

"My emotions are flying too high at present to make a rational decision. I need time to think, to contemplate the best course."

To determine if I dare trust ye ever again.

"I shall give ye my answer when I return from Edinburgh."

9

Edinburgh
April 1720

Sitting at her dressing table, Mayra cracked the green wax seal. She managed to wait until she was alone in her chamber to read Logan's most recent letter. If only he'd made this much effort to write her before.

The weeks apart hadn't lessened her love for the rogue, more fool she.

The foolscap crackled softly as she unfolded the paper, then ran her fingertips over the crisp page. He'd touched this same surface with his strong, callused hands.

If she closed her eyes, she could still feel his fingers trailing across her cheek. She touched her mouth. And feel his firm, warm, wonderful lips upon hers.

Her eyes misted, and she released a ragged sigh as she slowly opened them.

My Dearest Mayra,

I pray this letter finds ye well, at least in form, if not spirit. I'm not surprised ye haven't responded to my previous missives, but I shan't give up so easily. I believe with all my heart we are meant to be together. Please allow me to prove myself to ye.

I wrote ye a poem. I ken women like such things.

My Love
Eyes the color of summer sky
Fair skin smooth and pearly white
Bowed lips, plump and strawberry red
Hair shimmering moonbeam bright

Yer faithful, loving, humble servant,
L

A smile twitching the corners of her mouth, Mayra slowly refolded the letter before adding it to the growing stack in her dressing table's drawer.

Poetry wasn't Logan's forte, but she adored him for the effort.

Skin pearly white, indeed.

A glass of sparkling wine in hand and one chain mail-covered shoulder propped against a marble column, Logan adjusted his itchy black mask for the umpteenth time as he scrutinized the ballroom, paralleled on two sides by gilded mirrors.

Seeking Mayra, he gulped down the tepid wine and swung his gaze toward the doors leading to the garden.

Too cold to venture out there tonight, even if a smattering of spring color dotted the well-ordered beds.

Still, he had a groom with a white horse waiting

before the mansion.

Just in case...

His gaze roved the crowd once more. For the tenth? Twentieth time?

Where was she? Coburn said Mayra wore a medieval maiden's gown of the palest blue adorned with silver netting.

Over four weeks had passed since she'd left Logan standing in The Dozing Stag, wondering if he'd truly destroyed his only chance at love and happiness. More than thirty sleep-deprived nights, flopping about his lonely bed, pummeling himself with recriminations.

He'd written her twice weekly, something he should've done long before.

In those missives, he'd apologized over and over, told her of his love, his plans for their future, and he begged her to give them a chance, to forgive him. He'd even written a sorry excuse for a poem.

She hadn't responded.

Not to a single correspondence.

Had she even received the missives?

He'd rather believe she hadn't than that she'd

ignored his letters.

As hers had been unheeded for months—no years.

Finally, unable to lounge about Lockelieth any longer without going *aff his heid* from frustration, his mind constantly straying to Mayra, Logan decided on a new course.

One that might fail, but which wouldn't have him twiddling his thumbs and moping about the keep. He must prove himself to her. Somehow convince her he'd never be so bloody stupid or deceitful again.

He searched the crowded room for the umpteenth time.

Guests in an enormous variety of costumes from creative to ridiculous—was Lord Fowler supposed to be a chicken or a turkey?—stepped in time to a Scottish reel or gossiped in small clusters, wine or punch glasses clasped in their gloved hands.

Others—mostly shy wallflowers and drowsy elderly dames—perched in the chairs lining the room's one end. And still more revelers wandered the perimeter, their countenances intense and searching.

Is that how he looked?

Almost desperate and yet hopeful too?

Did they, too, seek a beloved?

Or perhaps, their love unrequited, they merely sought a glimpse of the object of their affection?

Coburn swore he'd observed Mayra dancing a strathspey earlier, but although Logan had kept a hawk's eye on the milling throng, he'd seen nary a glimpse of a female with moonlight threaded through her locks, an enchanting pixyish smile on her rosy mouth, and the sky dancing in her merry blue eyes.

"Ye're moonin', cousin. I should dub ye Sir Dour, Knight of the Gloomy Realm." Coburn chuckled as he once again eyed Logan's costume up and down.

A bland look was Logan's only response to his cousin's needling.

"I still canna fathom why ye're dressed as a knight. Every time ye move, ye clink and clank worse than a black tinker's wagon. How do ye propose to dance, or piss for that matter, in that contraption?" He flicked a long finger at Logan's armor, mirth cavorting in his merry gaze, visible through his mask's eye slits.

A skeptical brow elevated, Logan eyed his

cousin's swashbuckler's attire, his dark red hair held in place by a dashing blue scarf.

"At least I chose a respectable profession."

"Ach, trust me, cousin, the lasses dinna always want a respectable chap. Sometimes they want a *mon* to scoop them into their arms, whisk them away, and steal a kiss." Smirking, he gave a wicked wink. "And sometimes sample a wee bit more of their bountiful charms, too."

"Ever the romantic. Some women do like being treated with respect and reverence, ye ken." Logan's droll response earned him a whoop of laughter.

"Dear cousin, ye are completely, absolutely besotted." Coburn's grin couldn't be described as anything other than gloating.

"Just ye wait, Coburn. Yer day may come yet," Logan said. "And if it does, I'll be right there mockin' ye, rubbin' yer nose in yer warmer affections."

Coburn threw his hands across his chest in theatric horror. "Bite yer tongue. My day will never come. Unlike ye, I'm no' obligated to produce an heir."

"I assure ye, my determination to win Mayra,

despite my earlier stupidity, has nothin' whatsoever to do with obligation." Casting his cousin a look just this side of exasperated, Logan stretched his neck and scoured the crowd.

Probably look like a damned crane.

A burgundy-and-gold liveried servant passed by, and Coburn snatched two more glasses of wine. After passing one to Logan, he took a deep swallow, then made a face. "Weak as milk. I ken for a fact, McCullough has a stash of whisky and French brandy in his study. What say we help ourselves to a tot or two?"

Logan surveyed the ballroom once more.

No Mayra.

Mayhap she'd heard he was here and had fled?

His stomach and heart dove to his booted feet, heavier and swifter than an anchor chucked over a schooner's side met the river's bottom.

Still, he wasn't ready to quit the field just yet.

"Ye go on ahead. I'm goin' to wander around and try to find my betrothed."

How he adored saying that, declaring she was his.

Even if it were only true for a short while longer.

Tonight, he'd know her preference, one way or the other.

Unless Mayra had truly left already.

Odin's toenails.

He should've considered the possibility. However, if she had indeed departed, he had his answer. Just not the one he'd wanted.

"Never thought the day would come, that ye'd be ballocks over chin in love. And honestly, I'm utterly terrified that I, too, may someday become so ensnared." Coburn gave a much exaggerated shudder. "Aye, a stiff quaff is most definitely in order."

With a jaunty wave, he headed toward one of the entrances, but halfway to his destination, he veered toward a raven-haired female pirate.

Lips twitching, Logan pointed his gaze ceilingward and shook his head.

Mayhap sooner than ye think, cousin.

Methodically strolling the ballroom's border, he kept watch for a vision in blue and silver. Asking acquaintances if they'd seen her would only raise questions and possibly make things more awkward for Mayra, so he elected to keep his own counsel.

Nonetheless, he'd been here a full thirty minutes without a single glimpse of her, and that didn't bode well.

He passed the terrace windows reflecting the glow of hundreds of candles, and after glancing through the panes and assuring himself no one loitered outside, except for the willing groom paid very well to stand with Logan's noble steed, he continued on to the card room.

He swiftly perused the occupants.

Not there either.

Hands on his hips, he blew out a frustrated breath.

Devil it.

Where *was* his love?

In a carriage, trundling to the Windlespoons' manor?

Was he truly too late?

The fine hairs on his nape stood up as if electrified, and he slowly turned around.

There Mayra stood, slightly uncertain, but beyond

exquisite at the top of the fan-shaped stairway. Someone had tamed her wild mane, and it hung to her waist in silky waves. A circlet of diamonds graced her forehead and the choker at her neck.

A dozen swains rushed to the bottom riser, all jabbering and posturing for her attention.

Jealousy, scorching and swift heated his blood.

A fleeting smile touched her mouth, but Logan didn't miss the discomfiture in her eyes.

She was wholly out of her element.

Striding across the marbled floor, his boots clacking and his armor jangling, he never took his attention from her.

Upon hearing his rackety approach, she turned her head, and a radiant smile of relief blossomed across her face.

She'd recognized him. Surely that meant something.

The bucks vying for her attention noticed her focus and turned disgruntled expressions his way.

One chap, dressed as a jester nudged another attired in...

A frog costume?

They both turned bland stares on Logan, smirking at his ill-fitting armor.

He pushed his way through her admirers, perhaps using his elbows a trifle more exuberantly than necessary.

A tall, striking Roman centurion sporting a beak-like nose and haughty countenance blocked the stairs. Surveying Logan's over-sized breastplate, he sneered.

"It appears you had difficulty finding a costume that fit," he said, his clipped British accent almost as austere as the brows rising impossibly higher on his forehead. "Last minute decision to attend?"

"Ye might say that." Logan shrugged, his full attention focused on the vision floating down the stairs, her gaze locked with his.

Beak-nosed man noticed and tried to step in front of him. "Who are you, sir, that you so brazenly stare at our fair Miss Findlay?"

"I can answer that, Lord Strudwick." Mayra's musical, husky voice drew the men's attention. "He is Logan Rutherford, laird of Lockelieth Keep. And he is my betrothed."

Hope sprang anew in Logan's chest.

Did she mean it?

He stepped forward and offered her his arm.

Resting her fingertips upon his forearm, Mayra swept the peeved men a winsome smile.

"If ye'll excuse us?" She bent her head at a conspiratorial angle. "We've wedding details to discuss."

Grumbling their disappointment, the men wandered away.

Logan raised her hand, and searching her eyes, kissed her fingertips. "Never have I beheld such magnificence. I wanted to punch them all for daring to look upon yer loveliness."

Head tipped, she searched his face. "I'm surprised to see ye, Logan. Ye didna mention coming to Edinburgh in yer letters."

Ach, so she had received them. "I couldn't stay away. I had to see ye, to beg ye again to forgive me."

"We're garnering attention." Her bright gaze strayed beyond him.

He cast a quick glance over his shoulder. "I dinna care. Did ye mean what ye said? That we've a weddin' to plan?"

His heart stuttered in anticipation of her answer.

"Aye." She blushed, pink tinting her porcelain cheeks. "Don't mistake me. I'm still thoroughly miffed at ye, but I love ye. And given a choice of life with ye and without, I choose ye. I would like to start over and begin our relationship anew, with both of us committed to being totally honest with each other."

Logan's grin would've lit the heavens; he was positive.

He didn't deserve her mercy or forgiveness, but he'd accept them with the gratefulness of a dying man given another chance at life.

"Well, then my beloved Scots lass, I've never had the opportunity to propose to ye."

He sank onto one knee, his armor clinking and clanking, then took one of her hands in his.

Her eyes rounded and a tremulous smile framed her mouth when she caught on to what he was about.

God help him to regain his feet with a measure of

decorum.

The grand entrance and the ballroom doorways filled with gaping onlookers, but Logan paid them little mind. A gradual hush spiraled outward from where he knelt, and Mayra smiled down at him, love shining in her slightly misty eyes.

"Mayra Effie Lilias Findlay, will ye take this flawed, unworthy Highlander who adores ye and give him another chance to prove to ye, how utterly remarkable, delightful, and exceptional ye are?"

Her smile softened even more. "Oh, aye. I shall. I shall."

She nodded, her hair swirling about her shoulders and her smile lighting her entire countenance, as he managed to stand with her assistance.

How in Hades did men fight battles wearing this device?

"I'm so happy," Mayra said. "If there weren't so many people watching us, Logan, I'd kiss ye."

"I've nae such compunction." He swept her into his arms, and kissing her full on the mouth, trooped to the manor's exit.

A startled butler yanked the door open.

The clattering of guests' shoes, the swishing of their clothing, and the soft buzz of frenetic whispering echoed behind Logan as he continued marching down the stairs.

"I'll be jiggered!" Coburn said, clapping in approval. "Well done ye, cousin."

Logan sent him a smug grin.

Mayra giggled when she saw the horse. "Sir Knight, do ye mean to whisk me away on yonder steed?"

Logan set her down, just long enough to vault into the saddle.

Actually given the unaccustomed armor encasing him, it was more of a noisy, awkward, wholly undignified arse in the air clamor, assisted by the widely grinning groom.

Logan tossed the amused chap a coin, which he promptly pocketed before cupping his hands for Mayra to step into. "M'lady?"

Light as a nymph, she deftly positioned herself sideways before Logan on the saddle. Wrapping her arms about his waist, she laid her head against his chest. "I believe we've caused a scandal."

He lowered his lips to hers once more, savoring the sweetness of her mouth she readily opened to him.

"I hope so, my love. I do hope so."

Epilogue

Lockelieth Keep
October 1720

Mayra balanced her chin on her cupped hands as Logan slept beside her. The fire she'd stoked after checking on Isla, cast long, frolicking shadows across their bed and onto the walls behind it.

The lass had come to live with her and Logan a month ago, when her mum remarried and couldn't be bothered with her daughter any longer. Sometimes the poor waif cried out in her sleep, as she had tonight, and Mayra comforted her until she fell asleep once more.

His bare, muscled chest, sprinkled with deep russet hair, tempted too much, and Mayra played her fingertips through the crispy curls.

He cracked an eye open.

"My lady wife, are ye starin' at me again while I slumber?"

She did so often, and it had become a jest between them.

"Aye. I am." Mayra grinned and kissed his chest.

She'd never tire of touching him.

In one deft movement, he pulled her atop his sculpted body, then cupped her bottom in his big hands as he nibbled the sensitive arc where her shoulder met her neck.

"Lasses who wake their husbands from a sound sleep must pay a fine."

"No' so bad a price to pay."

She angled her head to give him better access, her hair forming a curtain about their heads and shoulders.

His manhood stirred beneath her belly, and she nipped his collar bone in anticipation of their joining. He groaned and lifted his pelvis, his desire thick and hot beneath her, but she wasn't ready to end their foreplay just yet.

"Did I tell ye I finally received a response to my petition from King George?" She gasped when Logan brushed his palm across her breasts, lingering for a moment on each nipple.

"Did ye, now?"

He didn't seem the least interested, apparently finding her breasts more fascinating then news from their monarch.

"Aye," She managed on a breathless gasp. "Only this afternoon."

Yesterday, actually. The clock had chimed three a bit ago.

Logan stroked the length of her spine, his rough fingertips brushing across her bottom and upper thighs before making the reverse trek.

"And what did our illustrious Majesty say after all these months? That ye dinna have to wed me after all, lass?"

The heavy bedcovers rustled as he thrust his hips against her mons again, and she swallowed a moan of longing, then giggled when he flipped her onto her back.

"Actually, he said ye did have to honor the contract, else ye'd have to forfeit my dowry. To him."

"He didna." Eyes half-closed, Logan stopped his sensual onslaught and gave one short shake of his head. "The greedy sot."

"My thoughts as well. He'd have apoplexy if he kent we've already found copper in the mine." She nuzzled his hairy chest, drawing in a deep breath, savoring his masculine scent.

Logan waggled his eyebrows, a confident grin tilting his mouth.

"Do ye suppose he'll be peeved that the deed is done and that ye're increasin' already?"

"Och, serves him right."

"Ye ken, I'd willingly forfeit it all—Lockelieth, the mines, everythin', if that were the cost he demanded to keep ye at my side." Logan raised himself up onto his elbows and rained gentle kisses across her forehead, nose, cheeks, and finally, a tender kiss upon her waiting mouth.

"I ken." Mayra entwined her arms about his neck and opened her legs to the gentle, insistent nudge of his knee between her thighs.

"I'd do the same for ye, without a second thought or a speck of remorse, because I love ye above all else."

"And I love ye, Mayra." As Logan slid his length home, he lowered his mouth to an inch above hers.

"Let me show ye how verra much, for the rest of our lives."

About the Author

USA Today Bestselling Historical Romance Author, Collette Cameron, pens Scottish and Regency Romances featuring rogues, rapscallions, rakes, and the intrepid damsels who reform them. Mother to three and self-proclaimed Cadbury chocoholic, she's crazy about dachshunds, cobalt blue, and makes her home in Oregon with her mini-dachshunds. You'll always find animals, quirky—sometimes naughty—humor, and a dash of inspiration in her novels.

Explore **Collette's worlds** at
www.collettecameron.com!

Join her **VIP Reader Club** and **FREE newsletter**.
Giggles guaranteed!

FREE STARTER LIBRARY: Join Collette's **The Regency Rose™ VIP Reader Club** to get updates on book releases, cover reveals, contests and giveaways she reserve exclusively for email and newsletter followers. Also, any deals, sales, or special promotions are offered to club members first. She will not share your name or email, nor will she spam you.

https://collettecameron.com/TheRegencyRoseVIPClub

Follow Collette on BookBub
https://www.bookbub.com/authors/collette-cameron

From the Desk of Collette Cameron

Dearest Reader,

I ventured into unknown territory with ***To Love a Highland Rogue***, which was initially written to be a part of ***The Forbidden Highland's*** anthology. My previous books have all been set in the late 1700s and early 1800s, but this Scottish romance takes place earlier. I discovered I loved the era so much, I wanted to write an entire series, and so my Heart of a Scot series came to be.

There are elements of that time period that might be a bit hard for the modern reader to grasp. For instance, children being contracted to wed by their parents. Forced and arranged marriages were common, but as with any true romance, Mayra and Logan fell in love and have their happy ending. Coburn's story is next up in the series, and I have a feeling, he's in for a shock or two.

If you're a fan of Scottish Romances, be sure to take a peek at my Highland Heather Romancing a Scot series. I've included a chapter of the first book in the series, *Triumph and Treasure.*

Please consider telling other readers why you enjoyed this book by reviewing it at the site where you purchased it. Not only do I truly want to hear your thoughts, reviews are crucial for an author to succeed. **Even if you only leave a line or two, I'd very much appreciate it.**

So, with that I'll leave you.

Here's wishing you many happy hours of reading, more happily ever afters than you can possibly enjoy in a lifetime, and abundant blessings to you and your loved-ones.

Collette Cameron

Connect with Collette!
www.collettecameron.com

Follow her on:
Twitter @Collette_Author
Bookbub.com/authors/collette-cameron
Facebook.com/collettecameronauthor
Instagram.com/collettecameronauthor
Amazon.com/author/collettecameron.com
Goodreads.com/collettecameron
Pinterest.com/colletteauthor

Enjoy the first chapter of

Triumph and Treasure

Highland Heather Romancing a Scot, Book One

Boston, Massachusetts, Late March 1818

Angelina Ellsworth—no, she was Mrs. Moreau now—cast her husband of six hours a look of adoration as he escorted her across the marble floor of the luxurious Plaza Hotel. She resisted the urge to dance a giddy jig.

She really was married.

She tried not to gawk at the immense glittering eight-foot crystal chandeliers, marble pillars and life-size, almost nude—er, make that entirely nude—

statues of mythical gods and goddesses. Cherubs, their chubby feet and legs immersed in water, edged a towering fountain burbling in the center of the lobby.

"Rather dazzling, is it not, *chérie*?"

Her gaze flashing to Charles's amused one, she flushed. She'd been craning her neck, staring at the *trompe l'oiel* ceiling depicting gods and other immortals, also bare as Norfolk dumplings. Papa would have been scandalized. Nudity, mythical gods, vulgar displays of wealth. Blasphemous.

She released a happy sigh.

And utterly splendid.

If Papa had been alive, he never would have consented to Charles courting her. Papa had been determined she marry a gentleman of his ilk. A staid, devote, *boring* fellow. Better yet, a man of the cloth. And with dowries the size of thimbles, Angelina and her sisters had few suitors, let alone young, debonair ones such as Charles.

Thank goodness, Mama entertained her own ideas, and after Papa's passing, voiced and implemented them with complete disregard as to what her husband would have preferred. A romantic at heart, once Mama realized Angelina loved Charles, she consented to the match.

Angelina shook off her dreary thoughts. This was her wedding day. A rush of excitement caused her to breathe quicker.

At ten o'clock this morning, she and Charles exchanged their vows before a crowd of well-wishers. After a modest breakfast and reception at her childhood home, Endicott Hall, they'd departed Salem.

"Here's your room key, sir."

The skeleton key clinking on the countertop reigned in Angelina's ruminations.

"Thank you." Charles slipped the key into his coat pocket before taking her arm. "Is the room prepared?"

"Yes, sir. Everything is as you requested." The clerk smiled. "May I offer my congratulations, Mr. and Mrs. Moreau?"

"Thank you." Angelina and Charles spoke simultaneously.

He patted her arm, giving her a crooked smile. Her stomach did that peculiar flip-flop it did whenever he smiled at her.

In two days, they'd sail to the Continent for a lengthy honeymoon in Italy by way of France. Prior to meeting Charles, Angelina only dared hope that perhaps someday she might visit her aunt and uncle, the Duke and Duchess of Waterford, in England. She'd never met them. Aunt Camille was her mother's twin, and they exchanged correspondences on occasion.

Angelina cast Charles a sidelong peek as he guided her toward the curved staircase. It had been three months since this splendid man entered in her life.

If it hadn't been for Mama's insistence that Angelina attend the Dennison's Christmas ball, she might never have met him. She hadn't wanted to attend, aware her father's cohort, horrid yellow-toothed Abraham Stockton, would be there. The paunchy man always smelt of garlic and sweat. And he was five and forty, if he was a day.

Despite Mama's adamant refusal to allow him to call upon Angelina, he'd been trying to court her for three years, since she turned seven and ten. Mama claimed the man was dicked in the nob. Angelina suspected, had he lived, Papa would have arranged a match between her and Mr. Stockton. She shuddered at the notion.

She'd been hiding from him in a curtained alcove at the Dennison's when a man darted into the enclosure.

Unaware Angelina huddled on a sofa tucked in the corner, he peeked between the heavy velvet panels, muttering, "A more persistent match-making *maman* I've never encountered, and four plainer, pudgier mademoiselles . . ."

Angelina erupted into laughter. "Mrs. Twiggels and the quartet, I'd wager."

Charles spun around, peering into the shadowy nook. He chuckled, a wonderful low rumble deep in his chest. "Twiggels? Please tell me you jest."

Yes, indeed, God had been smiling on her that evening, for Charles had arrived in Massachusetts that very day, brought to Salem on business. He was only at the ball by chance, his business associate having received an invitation and insisting Charles join him for the festivities.

Angelina swept Charles another love-filled gaze. His lips turned into a devilishly wicked smile, and the glint smoldering within his tawny eyes caused her heart to patter in anticipation.

With his black hair and high cheekbones, he cut such a dashing figure. The navy blue of his coat enhanced his unusual brandy-colored eyes and emphasized the breadth of his shoulders. Shoulders she itched to feel beneath her fingers.

Despite her gloves, her palms dampened. Angelina brushed her hands against her champagne-colored silk gauze gown, allowing herself to imagine Charles's hands caressing her.

Soon they would be.

They'd shared several fervent kisses during their short courtship, and once betrothed, he suggested they become more intimate. Raised by her zealot father, Angelina couldn't bring herself to sin *that* way. Not that she wasn't anticipating the marriage bed. She most definitely was.

She and Charles climbed the arched risers,

followed by four porters carrying their luggage. Their trunks had been sent on ahead to the ship. Charles's hand caressed her spine. A delicious tremor spiraled outward from where his palm lingered. She suppressed a slight gasp.

Something more than curiosity stirred, making her impatient for Charles's touches and kisses.

And he was a *most* skilled kisser.

A widower, forced at the tender age of twenty to marry a much older woman to save his family's estate, in the seven years since, he'd made a fortune in commerce.

Angelina held no doubts his handsomeness availed him of many a willing bed partner, though she wasn't supposed to know of such things. And if the Dennison's ball was an indication, women threw themselves at him. However, he had chosen her, and it astounded her.

He vowed at least a hundred times that he'd never loved another, and that Angelina would be his until the day he died. She'd no misgivings about his affection. A man couldn't pretend the warmth in his amber eyes or the husky timbre of his voice when he spoke of his adoration.

She pressed her fingers against the ruby and diamond ring encircling her finger.

Yes, this was real.

"Happy, *mon ange?*" Charles gave her waist a slight squeeze.

His angel? She smiled and nodded, releasing a contented, sigh. "Yes, blessedly and deliriously happy."

She'd found love. Something her parent's marriage lacked and hadn't been altogether certain existed outside her novels.

"Here we are." Charles's hand rested at the curve of Angelina's ribs, his thumb rubbing against her gown. She bit her lip to keep from giggling. He waited for the attendant to unlock their suite. The door swung open, revealing a room resplendent with roses of every imaginable shade.

Angelina stepped farther inside, then spun in a slow circle, her skirts swishing about her ankles. The heady perfume of a hundred blossoms permeated the air. She sniffed in appreciation. Surveying the chamber, she spied flowers in the adjoining bedchamber. She darted to the parted door.

After peering within, she sent a glance over her shoulder. "What in heaven's name?"

Speaking to the porters, Charles didn't hear her.

Untying the ribbon at her chin, she removed her bonnet. Her spencer followed. She placed both on the table beside the door, adding her reticule atop the pile. Angelina studied the bed dominating the room. A monstrous thing with carvings on the bedposts and along the canopy from which hung scarlet bed curtains, it was a blessed wonder the frame supported the oversized mattress.

She stepped closer, inspecting the engraved posts.

Oh my.

The etchings were of nude forms entwined in various acts of intimacy.

Good heavens.

Similar images of Greek and Roman gods adorned the walls and ceilings. The chamber was as wicked as Sodom and Gomorrah. For the first time since entering the dazzling hotel, she experienced a tinge of discomfit. She wandered to the bedchamber's entrance.

Charles finished speaking to the remaining attendant and passed the young man a coin.

The porter smiled widely. "Of course, sir. Right away."

He stepped into the corridor, then hesitated, staring at the luggage piled about the entrance. "Do you wish me to have a maid sent to unpack . . .?"

Charles shook his head. A strand of midnight hair fell across his forehead. "No, we're here only two nights. We sail the day after tomorrow. I'm sure my wife and I can manage."

He turned to wink at Angelina.

She grinned at him.

Incorrigible rogue.

But he was her rogue. He closed the door before crossing to her in several elongated strides. Sweeping her into his arms, he nuzzled her neck. She adored how she fit beneath his chin. At five feet eight inches, she stood taller than most woman of her acquaintance. Yet within Charles's embrace, she felt dainty and feminine.

Angelina laughed huskily. "My goodness, why the roses?"

"For you *mon ange* rose. I wasn't able to fill the room with angels, but roses, that I could arrange. I've imagined you naked, lying on a bed scattered with rose petals."

Should she be shocked? For the life of her she couldn't summon a jot of chagrin. My, she'd become scandalous since meeting Charles.

He stepped away from her, unbuttoning his cutaway coat. The gleam in his eye caused her pulse to do all manner of odd things. Surely he didn't intend to . . .

It was most improper during the daytime. Wasn't it? She glanced to the window, searching the horizon. The sky was enshrouded in a smoky violet-gray. Dusk had scarcely fallen.

Charles wound his arms around her once more, reining in her wayward thoughts. He kissed her like a man long starved. Curving her arms behind his neck, she returned the kiss.

He nudged his hips against her belly, his desire

evident. "I simply must have you now, *mon amor*. I cannot wait."

She hadn't expected he would be quite so eager to bed her-before dinner even. It thrilled and disconcerted her simultaneously.

"Help me with the hooks, will you?" She made to turn her back, needing his assistance to unfasten the gown.

"No, that shall take too long."

Before she knew what he was about, he scooped her into his arms. In two strides he reached the bed, then laid her upon the lush counterpane. Charles shoved her skirts to her thighs, and after fumbling with the falls of his trousers, parted her legs.

Apprehension swept her. "Charles, I'm not . . . This is so sudden, I don't . . ."

She gasped on a cry.

"Mon Dieu," he groaned against her neck.

Blinking back tears and biting her lip against the stinging, Angelina stared at a lurid picture on the wall. Was it supposed to hurt his much? Charles stiffened and gave a final moan before collapsing atop her.

That was it?

All the fuss was about *that*? Awash in disappointment and miffed at his callousness, she barely took note when he rose from the bed and fastened his trousers.

He chuckled, trailing a finger across her lips. "You resemble a wanton laying here with your breasts revealed, legs spread, and dress bunched to your hips."

Shame and humiliation surged through Angelina. She turned her face away, shoving the dress to her knees with one hand and tugging the bodice over her breasts with the other. She swallowed against the tears burning at the back of her throat.

How could he say that?

"*Chérie?*" Charles cupped her cheek, forcing her to meet his eyes. "I'm sorry, *mon amor*. I'm a selfish oaf. I promise, you, I'll take my time the next go round. You shall see how wonderful making love can be."

He bent and kissed her. Someone knocked on the outer door, then rapped again, this time more insistent.

"Ah, that must be our food." He gave her a boyish

grin. "I hope you don't mind. I requested an intimate dinner here rather than the noisy restaurant below."

After helping her off the bed, he placed another tender kiss on her lips. "I love you, *amoureux*." He buttoned his jacket, saying, "I'll get the door while you repair your appearance."

Whistling, he left the chamber, closing the door behind him. Repair her appearance? She would much rather take a lengthy bath liberally dozed with scented oil. She had been anticipating becoming a woman for weeks and truth to tell, it wasn't at all what she dreamed it would be.

Something sticky trickled down her thighs.

Angelina rushed to the bathing chamber. Dampening a cloth from the pitcher of water on the washstand, she made quick work of cleansing herself, grimacing at the blood on the linen. After cleansing away the evidence of her virginity and Charles virility, she smoothed her chemise and dress, shaking the fabric until the folds fell into place.

The pearl pendant above her breasts hung askew. She straightened the necklace, and then adjusted her bodice, wincing slightly. Charles had certainly been exuberant in his attentions. Mama had explained what to expect, still . . .

Angelina examined her face in the looking glass as she tidied her hair. Several curly tendrils had escaped the Grecian knot atop her head. Other than rosy lips and cheeks, she didn't appear different from the woman who had entered the chamber a few minutes ago.

Except, she was no longer an untried maid.

She hoped next time would be more . . . satisfying.

Making her way through the bedchamber, she hesitated. Men's voices were raised in anger in the other room.

How strange.

"Up to your old tricks I see, Pierre," said an unfamiliar slightly French accented voice.

Pierre? Angelina opened the door. She stopped short at the threshold.

The man before Charles was no servant. Sporting a thin mustache, the stranger stood attired in the latest fashion. From his gleaming Hessians and cream-colored pantaloons, to his jade green coat and knotted neckcloth, from which a jeweled stick pin glistened, he exuded quality.

He was profoundly handsome. And extremely angry.

Another man stood by the entrance. Much less refined, he grasped the handle of a gun tucked into his waistband. She slapped a hand to her mouth, trying to stifle the gasp that tore from her.

As one, the men's gazes came to rest on her. Charles's worried and angry, the rough fellow's, aloof, and the handsome man's, curious and *compassionate*?

"Charles, whatever is going on?" Angelina wrapped her arms about waist to calm her tumultuous stomach. Her husband's face had taken on a greenish hue. She feared he might cast up his accounts. He opened his mouth to speak. No sound emerged.

The mustached man shook his head disdainfully.

"Charles? How unoriginal." He bowed to Angelina. "Mademoiselle Ellsworth, allow me to introduce myself. I'm Jacques, Baron Devaux-Rousset."

Angelina didn't extend her hand. Instead, she tightened the grip around her middle. Pale, his lips pressed into a thin line, Charles glowered at the Frenchman. This man was no friend.

"My lord, did Charles not inform you? I'm Mrs. Moreau. We were married this morning. Please excuse my forwardness, but how are you acquainted with my husband, and who pray tell, is Pierre? Him?" She pointed at the surly man who continued to finger his weapon.

The brute smiled, a humorless curling of his lips.

Lord Devaux-Rousset speared Charles with an indiscernible glance before answering. "I'm his stepson, though, paradoxically, he is the same age as me."

Oh, the older woman Charles married. He hadn't mentioned she'd been a baroness or that she had children. Whyever was her son here? Boston was too far from France for Angelina to believe this was a chance encounter. Something was too smoky by far.

She sneaked Charles a sidelong glance. Why didn't he say something? He stood there seething with silent fury and glared daggers at the baron.

Angelina angled her head. "Charles told me of his marriage to your mother. I'm sorry for your loss."

For a moment, the baron's composure wavered. He gaped at her before turning a steely glower on Charles.

"*Vous avez dit que sa mère était morte?*"

Drat, she didn't speak French, but the baron had mentioned something about his mother's death. That much she gleaned. Perhaps she shouldn't have offered her condolences. The mourning period was over, had been for nine months. At least she thought that's what Charles had told her.

Or, perhaps it hadn't been that long, and that's why the baron was annoyed.

"Charles, are you not out of mourning?"

"*Merd*e," Charles muttered, staring at the floor and fisting his hands.

"There is a lady present, *imbécile*," the baron snapped. "Hold your foul tongue."

He turned his attention to Angelina. His expression softened. With a wave of his manicured hand, he indicated the ivory and gold striped sofa beside her.

"Mademoiselle, perhaps you should have a seat, and I'll explain."

Why did he insist on calling her mademoiselle? It was rather boorish. No, it was pointedly rude. "Thank you, no. I'd rather stand, my lord."

The baron regarded her for an extended moment. He gave a slight shrug. "As you wish."

He turned to the brute blocking the door. "Please wait in the hallway and deter any staff. I don't wish to be disturbed."

After scanning Charles contemptuously one final time, the baron's henchman gave a curt nod and exited the chamber.

Lord Devaux-Rousset sighed and slapped his beaver hat against his thigh. His gaze skimmed Angelina from her hair to her shoes, taking her measure. "You are lovely. I understand Pierre's fascination. Thank God, I arrived before he compromised you."

Angelina frowned. Was the man daft?

"Pierre? Who is Pierre? And how, in God's precious name, can my husband *possibly* compromise me?"

His voice very soft, and equally as gentle, Lord Devaux-Rousset murmured, "I sincerely regret having to tell you. The man you call husband is the well-known slave-trader, Pierre Renault."

He leveled Charles a blistering glare.

"And, I assure you, his wife, my *maman*, was very much alive when I left France."

Made in the USA
Lexington, KY
14 October 2017

Heart of a Scot

A Scottish lass determined to end her betrothal...

As an infant, Mayra Findlay's hand was pledged in marriage. So closely has her virtue been guarded, she's never been permitted a beau—has never even flirted with a man. Though she's repeatedly written her negligent intended—a man she's seen but once over a decade ago—asking him to break the agreement, her requests have gone unanswered. However, after a chance encounter with a dashing rogue who sets her pulse and imagination cavorting, Mayra initiates a scheme that's sure to force her affianced to call off their union.

The laird who must make her his at all cost...

Logan Rutherford, Laird of Lockelieth Keep, has no intention of taking to wife the lass a long-dead king decreed Logan should wed as a lad of six. But when he learns his late father spent the portion of Mayra Findlay's dowry entrusted to his care, and left him a near bankrupt estate, Logan's plans to petition the king for a reprieve are ruined. He needs Mayra's remaining dowry to save his beloved Lockelieth. Determined to know just what type of woman's he's reluctantly taking to wife before they exchange vows, he assumes his cousin's identity; a decision that soon has him snared in a tangled web of deceit.

USA TODAY BESTSELLING AUTHOR

COLLETTE CAMERON

USA TODAY
BESTSELLING AUTHOR

BLUE ROSE ROMANCE™

COLLETTE CAMERON

COLLETTECAMERON.COM

ISBN 9781944973506

90000 >

9 781944 973506